AMG

11-19

D0938359

NO LONGER
PROPERTY OF PPLD

The Marquis
Takes a Bride

The Marquis Takes a Bride

Marion Chesney

G.K. Hall & Co. • Chivers Press
Thorndike, Maine USA   Bath, England

This Large Print edition is published by G.K. Hall & Co., USA
and by Chivers Press, England.

Published in 1999 in the U.S. by arrangement with Signet,
a division of Penguin Putnam, Inc.

Published in 1999 in the U.K. by arrangement with the author.

U.S. Hardcover 0-7838-8777-9 (Romance Series Edition)
U.K. Hardcover 0-7540-3969-2 (Chivers Large Print)
U.K. Softcover   0-7540-3970-6 (Camden Large Print)

The text of this Large Print edition is unabridged.
Other aspects of the book may vary from the original edition.

Set in 16 pt. Plantin by Minnie B. Raven.

Printed in the United States on permanent paper.

British Library Cataloguing-in-Publication Data available

Library of Congress Cataloging-in-Publication Data

Chesney, Marion.
    The marquis takes a bride / Marion Chesney.
      p.   (large print)   cm.
    Originally published: New York : Signet, [1987], c1980, in series:
    Signet Regency romance.
    ISBN 0-7838-8777-9 (lg. print : hc : alk. paper)
    1. Large type books.   I. Title.
    PR6053.H4535 M33   1999
    823′.914 21—dc21   99-044278

To my friend, supporter
and helper, Madeline Trezza,
with much love.

Chapter One

Runbury Manor, home of Lord Charles and Lady Bemyss, had been designed by Robert Hooke in the seventeenth century and some uncharitable people said it had not been cleaned since.

It seemed, indeed, a fitting home for Lord Charles' pack of senile and bad-tempered old hounds since it smelled like a kennel. Elderly dogs lay gasping and panting in front of the fire in winter and snored in various Chippendale chairs in the summer, only rousing themselves to nip some passing guest.

Lord Charles had once explained to his friends and neighbors that since he himself could no longer follow the hunt and preferred to take his ease in a comfortable chair, then it was only fitting that his old friends of the hunt — the ancient remnant of his pack of hounds — should do likewise.

His lady Priscilla was equally devoted to the smelly animals, often preferring to talk to them rather than to any human being. The dogs understood so much more.

The couple would have been perfectly happy had they not been burdened with one human responsibility in the shape of their granddaughter, Jennie.

Jennie's parents had been taken by the cholera when she was still a baby and she could not remember them at all. She had been brought up by her grandparents, who were strict in some things and very lax in others.

She had been spared the rigors of an education, Lord Charles holding to the old-fashioned view that a female with an uneducated mind was a rare and beautiful thing, yet her social training had been severe. She knew how to curtsy with grace, how to manage a train, how to use a fan of any size, how to compliment a gentleman on his taste in snuff and how to listen to long and boring dissertations on hunting and agriculture with wide-eyed interest. Outside the Manor, however, she could run wild as she pleased and ride for miles around without the escort of a groom.

In the house, her duties were to help her grandmother in the still room and to eat everything on her plate at table. Any food left uneaten would be served to her at the next meal and, should she not eat it then, at the meal after that. She was taught to practice that cheese-paring economy so peculiar to the English aristocracy. Old clothes were never to be thrown away unless they were in rags and Jennie became an adept needlewoman — although she had little time to spend on her own clothes. When she was not sewing "white work" in long seams with all the mysterious rites of counter-hemming, running and felling, top-sewing and pointing, she was kept busy at her embroidery frame producing pictures in tent or tapestry stitch.

Provided she obeyed these rules of the house, her grandparents treated her with the same impatient kindness that they used to give their dogs when they were puppies.

In this unlikely atmosphere, Jennie bloomed like the rose. She had a mass of glossy black hair, a little heart-shaped face, wide hazel eyes and a petulant, at times willful, mouth. She had on occasion very pretty manners, a good deal of intelligence despite her lack of education, but was unfortunately inclined to sulks and temper tantrums. It was not because her grandparents were in any way indulgent, in fact they hardly noticed whether she was in a good mood or not, but she had been petted and indulged by her first cousin, Guy, for quite a number of her formative years.

Jennie had been in love with Guy since the days when she could only toddle after him. Guy was some five years older than Jennie, a slim young man of medium build with fair curly hair and an engaging boyish expression. He followed the sporting fashion of the Corinthians and ran around London with a set of wild young men who would have shocked Jennie to the core could she have seen them first-hand. But she only heard of their antics from Guy and thought that Guy and his circle must be the most dashing and elegant bloods in the world.

Jennie was, in fact, spoiled through neglect. Although she was fed and clothed, she was often lonely and had no books to pass the weary hours. She was often unsure of herself and had no one but Guy to turn to, her grandparents never understanding a word she said, immersed as they were in the narrow channel of their own lives. And like all neglected children, Jennie would throw scenes and temper tantrums as the only way she knew to satisfy her craving for love and attention.

Guy would soothe her and pet her and train her up in his own cynical worldly philosophy. And with only Guy to listen to her, Jennie grew more and more dependent on the young man for comfort and advice.

Guy was a regular visitor to the Manor. Like Jennie, his parents were dead. He lived in comfortable lodgings in St. James, but found the Manor a useful retreat from duns and creditors. He never failed to try to borrow money from Lord Charles, although he was hardly ever successful, Lord Charles becoming unaccountably deaf when anyone so much as hinted that his lordship should even part with a farthing.

He also enjoyed Jennie's uncritical adoration and in return brought her presents, told her there was no one in London to match her beauty and also tried to instill into her young brain his own peculiar moral code. Jennie, now on the eve of her eighteenth birthday, believed that one could do almost anything one liked provided one was not found out. Being found out, Guy would say, was a heinous crime. Marriage, Jennie learned, was the best future for a woman — not because she should fall in love and wish to have children, but because she would be free from the restrictions imposed on a single girl and be immediately able to set up a flirt. Women who were faithful to their husbands, Guy had told her, were the women who were too plain to catch the eye of anyone else.

And Jennie would drink in all this and believe every word. Having a lover, in Jennie's mind, was simply having someone to flirt and intrigue with, as she flirted and intrigued with Guy.

She was walking in the gardens of the Manor, hoping Guy would arrive in time for her birthday as he had promised, when she heard her grandfather's peremptory bark echoing through the open windows of the Blue Saloon, "Jennie, fetch your grandmother and bring her here. We want to talk to you."

Jennie looked startled. Her grandparents hardly ever wanted to see her about anything — anything, that is, that would involve the presence of both of them.

Her grandmother, she knew, would be in the still room and so she made her way there, secretly beginning to hope that her grandparents had actually, for once, bought her a birthday present.

Lady Priscilla was weaving around the still room with a vague sweet smile on her face. She had been making ice by putting equal parts of ether and water in a metal jug and then applying an air pump to the mixture. As usual, she had forgotten to open the little window in the still room and had knocked herself silly with the ether fumes.

With the ease of long practice, Jennie tugged open the window, placed a cover over the jug, stoppered the ether and supported her grandmother from the room.

Once they had reached the great hall, Lady Priscilla had recovered enough to straighten her cap and ask Jennie in an impatient voice what it was she wanted.

"Grandfather wants me to bring you to the Blue Saloon," said Jennie.

"Oh . . . yes . . . that," said Lady Priscilla, banging the side of her head with her hand to bring her weak eyes back into focus. "Most important, my dear. Follow me."

Jennie meekly followed her grandmother into the Blue Saloon, a great room which looked out onto the shaggy lawns at the front of the house. A few threadbare rugs holding stands of spindly tables and chairs were dotted like islands here and there on the expanse of sanded floor. The Bemyss ancestors stared down from their blackened canvases and dingy gold frames. Several clocks ticked away busily, set at every hour but the right one, and at least six dogs snored and wheezed and whooped as they chased rabbits in their sleep.

Lord Charles looked up as they came into the room.

He was a heavily built man with a florid face and rather protruding pale blue eyes. He was wearing a powdered wig, slightly askew, and was dressed like a farmer with his stocky, muscular legs encased in gaiters.

Lady Priscilla, by contrast, was pale and wispy and always seemed to have things trailing from her body — a thin, wispy gauze stole, a long limp glove held in one hand, limp streamers hanging from her unstarched cap or simply loose threads trailing from the hem of her gown.

"Sit down, Jennie," barked his lordship. All the comfortable chairs were occupied by dogs so Jennie took a hard camel-back chair near the window where the sweet, cool air of the evening blew in and banished the smell of dog — from that little area of the room at least.

"You're eighteen years old tomorrow, ain't you?" demanded his lordship, reluctantly putting down the latest edition of the *Sporting Magazine* ("Of the Transactions of the Turf, the Chase, and every other Diversion Interesting to the Man of Pleasure and Enterprize") and fixing his pale blue eyes on his granddaughter.

Jennie nodded and sat demurely on the edge of her chair with her hands in her lap. What present would they give her? Jewelry perhaps!

Then Lord Charles dropped his bombshell.

"You're to be betrothed tomorrow, Jennie. You're a lucky girl. He's a fine young man."

A delicate pink suffused Jennie's face.

"Guy," she breathed. "Oh, Grandpapa. I shall

remember this birthday until the day I die."

"What's that?" barked his lordship. "Guy? Don't be silly, girl. As if I would let you marry your first cousin. Country's going to rack and ruin and d'ye know why? Damned inbreeding, that's what it is. You're not marrying any first cousin, my girl, and producing a lot of totty-headed inbred brats. You're to marry Lord Cyril Chelmsford Branwell, fourth Marquis of Charrington. He's coming here tomorrow and we're signing the marriage settlements. So make sure you take a bath and put on some clean linen," added Lord Charles, who hardly ever did either himself.

"And if I refuse?" said Jennie in a dangerously quiet voice.

"What's that? Refuse? Nonsense. No question of it. Was all fixed by your dear Ma and Papa when you was in your cradle. You can't do nothing about it."

"I won't. I won't. *I won't,*" said Jennie, her voice rising to a scream and her little heels beginning to drum against the floor.

"Grandmama!" she stormed at that lady, "you cannot allow this to happen."

"But it has, my dear . . . or is . . . or will be," said Lady Priscilla vaguely. Her stomach gave a sudden violent rumble and she stared down at it in surprise.

"Did we eat dinner, my dear?" she inquired plaintively of her lord. "I cannot remember."

"We ate at four o'clock, you idiot," said Lord

14

Charles. "I remember it quite distinctly. It was a French stew of green peas and bacon."

"You're quite right, my dear," said his wife. "It was a very good pot beef with tomata catsup."

"Fool! French stew!"

"Oh, no, my love," replied his wife with maddening patience. "I remember now perfectly, don't I Caesar?" Caesar, a large wolfhound, gave a hiccup and a snore. "Dear doggie," cried Lady Priscilla. "Caesar says it was pot beef."

"Tcha! You've got windmills in your head."

"Enough! *Stop!*" cried Jennie desperately. "This is ridiculous."

"Quite right!" said Lord Charles in surprise. "Not often you agree with me, Jennie. As if that damned dog could remember anything. He can't remember *me*. Bit me the other day."

"You sat on him," pointed out his wife.

"I mean," shouted Jennie, "that I am *not* going to marry this Marquis. I am *not!*"

Lord Charles picked up his magazine.

"If you do not promise me that you will immediately cancel these absurd marriage plans, I . . . I shall *kill* myself," shouted Jennie.

"I have a very, very special bone for you, my love," murmured Lady Priscilla, patting Caesar's shaggy head.

Jennie threw up her hands in despair. "I shall hold my breath!" she yelled as a last resort.

There was a short silence while Jennie held her breath and Lady Priscilla murmured sweet nothings to the dog and Lord Charles read his magazine.

Suddenly Lord Charles put down his *Sporting Magazine* and looked across at his granddaughter, who was slowly turning purple.

"You know," he said in a kindly voice, "I ain't paid you much attention, Jennie. But you're a fine looking girl. Like to see a girl with a bit of color in her cheeks."

"Ooooh!" said Miss Jennie Bemyss, letting out her breath in a hiss of rage. "You do not care what becomes of me."

"I care," said a light voice from the doorway.

"Guy!" cried Jennie, throwing herself into his arms and gazing up at his tanned, handsome face. "I am so glad to see you. I was afraid you wouldn't come. Oh Guy they are going to marry me off to some Marquis!"

"Easy now," said Mr. Guy Chalmers, gently taking Jennie's clutching hands from his lapels. "Come and walk with me in the garden and tell me all about it."

"Good evening, sir," he said to Lord Charles. "I'm just going for a walk in the garden with Jennie."

"Oh, it's you, is it," said his lordship, ungraciously, and then his ears almost seemed to prick up as Guy rustled a paper in his pocket.

"I say," said Lord Charles, with rare enthusiasm, "you haven't, have you?"

"Yes, I have," grinned Guy, drawing a paper twist of chocolate drops from his pocket. He gave them to Lord Charles, who immediately began to munch happily, and then Guy tucked Jennie's hand in his arm and led her out to the garden.

Jennie had begun to sob quietly so he put an arm around her shoulders and walked her a little way from the house, waiting until she should recover enough to tell him her news.

The evening was very still. The dark layers of the cedars stood out against a pale primrose sky and the reed-choked waters of the once ornamental lake reflected a pale crescent of moon.

"Now, what is it?" asked Guy, "or are you going to cry all night? You look like a little rabbit when you cry, all pink nose and red eyes."

That had at least the effect of drying Jennie's tears and she proceeded to pour out the story of her betrothal into Guy's astonished ears.

When she had finished, he whistled silently. "The Marquis of Charrington," he said. "You could have done a lot worse, Jennie. He's as rich as Golden Ball and no end of a dandy."

"You-you t-told me that all d-dandies were effete," said Jennie, beginning to sob again.

"Yes, yes, forget that," said Guy impatiently. "But only think of the clothes and the jewels you'll have, Jennie. And you'll be in London and be able to see me an awful lot."

"But I thought . . . I mean . . . but I want to marry you!" she blurted out.

"It wouldn't answer," said Guy, smiling down at her and giving her a reassuring hug. "My

17

pockets are to let. Besides, I'm your first cousin. But, think of the freedom you'll have as a married woman."

Jennie only gave a pathetic little sob.

"Listen," urged Guy in rallying tones. "You can have me as your first flirt and we'll cut a dash. Smartest couple in town."

A note of real fear crept into her voice as she whispered, "But how will I be able to face living with a man I do not know? What of the intimate side of marriage?"

"That's easy," laughed Guy. "Chemmy Charrington — Chemmy's his nickname — has the reputation of being the sleepiest and most amiable man about town. Cares for nothing but his clothes. He probably don't want this marriage any more than you do. So you tell him it's a marriage of convenience and that you won't interfere with his pursuits. He'll agree to it, I'm sure."

"Oh, do you think so, Guy?" breathed Jennie with relief. "What does he look like?"

"He's quite old," said Guy. "About thirty-five. A great quiz of a fellow. All tricked out in foppish finery. He can't care much for the ladies or he'd have been married a long time ago instead of keeping to this odd betrothal. *Now* do you feel better?"

"Oh, *yes*. Oh, Guy, I do love you so," said Jennie, gazing worshipfully up into his face.

"Silly puss," he said in a teasing voice. He drew her into his arms and kissed her.

Guy had often kissed Jennie before but this time it was different. Her emotions overset by the shock of her betrothal, Jennie kissed Guy back with all the passion of a young woman.

When he finally drew away, he looked down at her in surprise. "Why little Jennie, how you've grown!" he said in a husky voice.

Then with a smile, he took her hand and began to lead her back to the house.

"All will be well," he told Jennie, "fashionable marriages have great advantages."

He gave a great cackle of laughter and stopped and looked down at her. "Believe me, my darling, there will be nothing like it!"

Chapter Two

Chemmy, fourth Marquis of Charrington, descended cautiously from his high perch phaeton, and stood looking thoughtfully at the ivy-covered front of Runbury Manor.

"Bad drains, John," he said to his groom. "Or perhaps they do not have any."

"Don't think so, my lord," grinned his groom with the easy familiarity of an old servant. "Folks say Lord Charles won't spend a penny on repairs so it stands to reason he won't have done much about the plumbing."

The Marquis took out a scented lace handkerchief and held it to his nose. "Perhaps there is no one at home," he said hopefully. "Our arrival does not seem to be expected. Ring the bell, John."

"Ain't got one," said the groom, banging on the knocker.

The door was cautiously opened to reveal one of the oldest footmen the Marquis had ever seen. He was stooped and wrinkled and dressed in the livery he must have worn as a young man.

Chemmy presented his card which the footman stared at for what seemed a very long time.

"This way, my lord," he finally said.

He led the way across a large, bare, dark hall,

flung open the double doors and ushered Chemmy into the Blue Saloon.

It was, thought the Marquis, rather like entering Madame Tussaud's waxworks museum. Lord Charles and Lady Priscilla sat side by side on hard upright chairs facing the doors. Like their footman, their clothes seemed to date from the late eighteenth century. Lord Charles wore a brocade coat, a full-bottomed wig and knee breeches. His lady was attired in a faded gold *sac* dress with long filmy threads drifting from it and on her head she wore a high, powdered wig, reminiscent of Madame Pompadour.

A very pretty young girl sat a little way from them on another hard chair. She at least was dressed in the current mode, wearing a sprigged muslin dress tied under her bosom with long pink ribbons. There was a tapestry frame in front of her and she sat very still, staring at the Marquis with her needle poised. A young man dressed in the Corinthian fashion stood rigidly at attention beside the fireplace.

The only comfortable chairs in the room were occupied by several somnolent dogs.

Four pairs of eyes stared fixedly at the Marquis.

The Marquis of Charrington was a very tall, powerfully built man and despite his great height he moved with easy, rather languid grace. He was dressed in correct formal attire, blue swallowtail coat with large steel buttons, worn open to reveal an embroidered cambric shirt, rose-colored waistcoat and intricate cravat. His legs were encased in skin-tight biscuit pantaloons and his hessian boots shone in the dusty sunlight permeating through the dingy windows. He carried his cane and curly brimmed beaver in one hand and a scented lace handkerchief in the other. His face was handsome but without much animation, his vivid blue eyes betraying only an expression of sleepy amiability. He had a high-bridged autocratic nose and his thick fair hair was cut in a fashionable Brutus crop.

"May I sit down?" he asked in a light, pleasant drawl. His blue eyes under their heavy lids surveyed the sleeping dogs. He crossed to the most comfortable chair, which was occupied by Caesar, and looked down.

"Get down, boy," he said to the dog in a pleasant voice which carried no hint of command. To the amazement of the watchers, Caesar immediately awoke, slid down from the chair and lay down on the rug.

The Marquis looked thoughtfully at the chair, he flicked the seat of it with his handkerchief, and then sat down. He lazily snapped his fingers to the waiting footman, handed him the soiled piece of lace and cambric and then looked thoughtfully at his future bride, who was staring at him open-mouthed. A strong smell of unwashed dogs and bad drainage assailed the Marquis' nostrils and, in front of Jennie's scornful eyes, he took out a small silver vinaigrette and held it to his nose.

"Fop!" said Jennie in a low voice to Guy. The amiable blue eyes looking in her direction suddenly seemed to narrow a fraction and, for one moment, Jennie was sure that he had heard her. But the next minute, he was looking just as sleepy and amiable as ever and she put it down to a trick of the light.

"Well," said Lord Charles in a jovial voice, "well, well, well, well, well." Everyone waited anxiously for him to go on but his lordship had fallen silent.

"Since no one is going to present me, I may as well present myself," said Jennie impatiently. "I, my lord, am Miss Bemyss."

"Charmed," murmured the Marquis, giving her a bow from his chair.

"This is my cousin, Mr. Chalmers . . . oh, I am doing things the wrong way around," exclaimed Jennie in pretty confusion. "I should have introduced my grandparents first . . . Lord and Lady Bemyss."

This time the Marquis rose to his feet, made Lady Priscilla a magnificent leg, and then sat down again.

A heavy silence fell upon the room, broken only by the whispering and ticking of the clocks.

Lord Charles cleared his throat noisily. "Hah!" he said. "Yes. Well."

Everyone looked helplessly at one another.

A diversion was created by the ancient footman who staggered forward bearing a small table laden with decanters, saffron cakes and Shrewsbury cakes.

Lady Priscilla appeared to come out of some very pleasant dream. The Marquis had bitten into a Shrewsbury cake and was staring at the remains of it in mild astonishment. "Is anything wrong?" she asked anxiously.

"No, indeed, ma'am," drawled Chemmy politely, letting the remains of the cake fall on the floor where it was eagerly gobbled up by Caesar, who was promptly sick.

Jennie took a cake from the plate offered to her by the footman and anxiously bit into it. It tasted as bitter as acid.

"Grandmama!" she choked. "What on earth is in this Shrewsbury cake?"

"Oh, dear," replied Lady Priscilla. "I was afraid it might not answer. Cook told me we had no caraway seeds left and I found some pretty seeds lying in the garden and I thought they would do just as well."

"Do not worry about it," said the Marquis. "The madeira is excellent."

"It *is?*" cried Lady Priscilla, with such surprise that the Marquis sniffed warily at his glass and wondered if she could possibly have made it herself.

Another long silence fell, this time broken by Guy. "It's deuced stuffy in here," he said. "I shall just take Jennie for a breath of air in the garden."

"No, you won't," barked Lord Charles, breaking into articulate speech for the first time.

24

"The young couple want to be alone to get acquainted." He got stiffly to his feet and held out his arm to his wife. Jennie nervously watched her grandparents leave the room.

Guy grinned down at her. "Best be off, Jennie." He lowered his voice to a whisper. "Don't forget . . ."

Jennie watched him go with her heart in her eyes. Then she reluctantly turned her attention to her betrothed.

"Do you wish this marriage?" asked the Marquis, in a pleasant, uninterested sort of voice.

Jennie looked at the large dandy with amused contempt. He was idly playing with his vinaigrette. She noticed that his cambric shirt was so fine it was nearly transparent and was embroidered with small bunches of forget-me-nots.

Take away his tailor, she thought in disgust, *and there would be nothing left but a great oaf.*

Summoning up her courage, she got to her feet and walked to stand in front of the Marquis. He politely rose from his chair and Jennie found to her dismay that she had to crane her neck to look up at him.

"My lord," she began, "I am sure you do not want this marriage any more than I do. It would be more dignified to cease this charade."

"Oh, no," remarked the Marquis with great good humor, "I don't consider it a charade at all. I wish to be married."

"Don't be ridiculous," remarked Jennie crossly, her temper rising. "You *can't* want to marry me. You don't even know me."

"That can be remedied."

"You can't *force* me to marry you," said Jennie, tears of anger beginning to sparkle in her large hazel eyes.

"No?" he said. "I can, in a way. We were legally betrothed when you were in your cradle. What frightens you about this marriage?"

"I do not love you," she said tremulously.

"Of course not," replied the Marquis with infuriating calm. "I do not believe in love at first sight. But I think we should deal together tolerably well. Come, my child, be reasonable. Would you not like to have your own establishment and fine clothes and a Season in London?"

"Y-yes, of course I would like that. But I cannot be your wife." Here she flung her head back in an overdramatic gesture worthy of that well-known actress, Mrs. Jordan . . . "unless you agree to a marriage of convenience, a marriage in name only."

He took so long to answer that her neck began to hurt and she had to relinquish her dramatic pose.

At last he said mildly, "I shall expect you to produce an heir at some time or another, you know. But you are very young and I am prepared to wait. At the beginning of our marriage, at least, you may lead your own life and follow your own amusements."

Jennie thought quickly. Oh, that she could marry Guy! But since she could not, surely it would be better to have a complaisant husband.

"Very well," she said sulkily, staring at the Marquis' waistcoat button.

He drew her gently to him and kissed her on the forehead.

"Why did you never marry before?" asked Jennie, suddenly shy.

"I must have been waiting for you," he answered lightly, "although my friends tell me I am married to my tailor."

If he cares only for clothes as Guy said, thought Jennie, beginning to relax, *he will have little time to think of his wife.*

Lord Charles and Lady Priscilla came into the room. They showed no surprise at the news that the couple were to go ahead with the wedding.

"Jennie has been trained to come to heel," said Lord Charles. "You should have no trouble with her."

"I hope, my lord," said Jennie sweetly, "that you will put a ring on my finger and not a collar around my neck."

"I shall supply you with whatever is necessary, I assure you," remarked the Marquis. "I think we should be married in three weeks' time."

"So soon," said Jennie faintly.

"Capital!" said Lord Charles.

"I see no sense in waiting," remarked the large Marquis. "After all, my dear, we have been betrothed for such a long time!"

The announcement of the Marquis' engagement to Miss Jennie Bemyss caused a certain flutter in London society, which had considered him a hardened bachelor.

One of the most astounded was his friend, Peregrine Deighton.

Peregrine was waiting impatiently for the Marquis on that gentleman's return from Runbury Manor. He was a small, dapper man with a small, military moustache and thick, pepper-and-salt hair. He had a broad forehead and large, slightly protruding brown eyes, a thin, straight nose and a small, severe mouth.

It had long been a source of wonder why the elegant and indolent Marquis should choose such an old-maid for a friend. For Mr. Deighton was inclined to be very prissy and had an embarrassing habit of speaking exactly what was on his mind at the time. But Peregrine had fought in the Marquis' regiment during the earlier years of the Peninsular Wars and the Marquis knew him to be gallant and brave, and sensitive to a fault, and repaid his little friend's loyalty with the same regard.

The Marquis entered the drawing room of his town house in Albemarle Street and looked with lazy amusement at the small, trim figure of Mr. Deighton, who was perched on the edge of a chair with the knob of his cane in his mouth.

He unplugged himself at the sight of the Marquis and immediately burst into speech. "Tell me it's not true!" he cried. "I could scarce believe my eyes when I read the *Morning Post*. You set out to tell the Bemyss family that you had no intention of getting married. What happened?"

"I must have fallen in love," remarked the Marquis languidly, stripping off his York tan driving gloves.

"You? Love? Nonsense!" exclaimed Mr. Deighton, who then, in his usual embarrassing way, plunged straight on into the reason for his distress over the forthcoming nuptials. "What will happen to all the fun we have?" he said. "What will happen to all the races and prize fights? The clubs and the opera? The days in the park? A wife will put a stop to all that!" He bounced up and down on the edge of the chair, his dapper little figure fairly quivering with distress.

"Down, boy! Down!" said the Marquis good-humoredly, and indeed his small friend did look rather like an agitated puppy who had just been refused a walk. "My affianced bride assures me that ours shall be a marriage of convenience. We shall go our separate ways until such times as I feel it necessary to produce an heir. If you go on in this heated fashion, Perry, the world will begin to wonder about my . . . er . . . tastes. Play me no jealous tragedies, Perry."

"You mean . . . you . . . me . . . people would think . . . *you* think," spluttered the enraged Perry. "Well, sirrah, if that is how you regard my devoted friendship . . . you may name your seconds!"

"I have absolutely no intention of getting up at dawn so that you can put a bullet through me," said the Marquis. "Take a deep breath and *think*, man . . . think how you sound."

"Jealous," replied Perry gloomily, with his usual forthright honesty. "Sorry, Chemmy. I'm jealous of a girl. But, damn, what kind of a girl is it that wants you in name only? Answer me that!"

"An enchanting, spoiled little minx," said the Marquis, smiling reflectively.

"And to add to the complications, Miss Bemyss is in love with her first cousin, Guy Chalmers."

"Not that loose screw," gasped Perry. "It's as well she can't marry him. Ruining servant girls and rolling old women in the kennel is more in his line."

"Tell me more," said the Marquis. "I do not know anything of Mr. Chalmers."

"He claims to be a Corinthian, which is simply an excuse for sloppy dress and the manners of the rabble," said Perry roundly. "He tries to emulate everything that set does, only he does it all badly. He boxes badly, shoots worse, wounded a gamekeeper at Lord Belling's shoot instead of hitting the bird he was supposed to, attends cock fights and bear battings at Islington in the most shady company, claims to be up to every rig and row in town, claims to be a lady's man and yet when he stayed at the Harrington's a month ago, 'tis said he got Mrs. Harrington's maid with child and then paid the girl to say that Mr. Harrington was the father, except that she confounded him by telling the truth . . . do you want to hear any more?"

"No," said the Marquis faintly. "I think I've heard enough."

"You say this marriage will not affect our friendship," went on his friend relentlessly. "But what of Mrs. Waring's 'friendship?' "

"Alice Waring knows my intentions towards her are, and always have been, strictly dishonorable," said the Marquis. "She will soon find another protector."

"Not her!" cried Perry. "I'm sure she thought you would marry her, sometime or other. After all, you haven't looked at another woman these past few years."

"You must be mistaken," said the Marquis, jolted slightly from his customary good humor. "I am not a fool, Perry. Had I thought that Alice expected more from me than the payment of her rent and jewels, I would have terminated that connection long ago."

"You ain't a fool," said Perry slowly. "But sometimes you can't see what's under your nose."

"Enough!" said the Marquis. "You will be best man at my wedding, I hope?"

"You mean you're really going through with it?"

"Oh, yes. I'm really going through with it."

"Then I shall stand by you," said Perry.

"Thank you," said the Marquis, and then surveyed his friend's brooding face. "I would appreciate your loyalty to my bride, Perry," he said quietly. "You are not to give her that piece of your mind you have so obviously reserved for her."

Perry flushed slightly. "Oh, well," he said sulkily. "But life won't be the same with Miss Jennie Bemyss around. Just you wait and see!"

After Perry had taken his leave, the Marquis sat for a long time, deep in thought. He had not intended to honor the betrothal. Although he had been aware from a long time back that it existed, he had never taken it very seriously. His parents had firmly believed in arranged marriages and had been close friends of Jennie's parents. Before their death, from one of the many typhoid epidemics which ravaged the English countryside, they had told the young Chemmy of the beautiful baby girl who would grow up to be his bride. He had put it far in the back of his mind, being for years too concerned with the managing of his estates which he had found in bad repair after a three years' absence in the Peninsular Wars.

As the years passed and no communication arrived from the Bemyss family, the Marquis had begun to think they had either forgotten about the whole thing or had found this "baby betrothal" as ridiculous as he did himself. That was until a letter had arrived from Lord Charles informing him bluntly of Jennie's approaching eighteenth birthday and firmly stating that the Marquis was expected to honor his dead parents' wishes.

So he had traveled to Runbury Manor to tell

Lord Charles, in the politest manner possible, that he had no intention of wedding some young miss who was little more than a schoolgirl.

Then he had seen Jennie. The Marquis smiled reflectively as he remembered the turmoil of his emotions on first seeing that wilful, infuriating, *darling* little beauty.

If he wished her infatuation for that unsuitable cousin to die out, then he would have to play his cards very carefully and keep a tight rein on his emotions. Miss Jennie Bemyss was going to need very careful handling indeed!

A little distance away in a slim house in Manchester Square, the news of the Marquis' engagement was received with more horror than even the sensitive and jealous Perry could muster.

Alice Waring was clutching the lapels of Guy Chalmers' coat and staring up into his face. "Tell me it's all a hum!" she cried. "Chemmy was to marry *me!*"

Guy disengaged himself and said cruelly, "You ain't the marrying kind. Lord Trace was keeping you before Chemmy, and before that, Richards."

"But I am good *ton*," sobbed Alice. "Everyone has liaisons."

"But not so blatantly as you," shrugged Guy. "Anyway, you're nearly thirty, Alice, and Jennie Bemyss is a gorgeous virgin of eighteen. Now, don't claw my eyes out, and let me think. I can help you."

Alice Waring dried her tears and looked at him

hopefully. She was a statuesque woman with a magnificent figure and a classically beautiful face with a pair of brown, almost oriental, eyes which surveyed the world with lazy sensuality from under a cloud of spun-gold hair.

She was the daughter of a bankrupt Irish peer and had repaired her fortunes by marrying a rich and elderly merchant, Mr. Josiah Waring, who had the good grace to take the smell of the shop and his unfashionable presence off into the other world two months after his marriage, leaving the grateful Alice with his very fashionable fortune. She had not wished to marry again, preferring to enjoy her freedom as a beautiful widow. She could not forget the straightened circumstances of her youth and made sure that her lovers were generous. She had not thought of marriage until the advent of Chemmy. The thought that she was no longer a girl, combined with her ambition to become a marchioness, had made her change her mind. She had convinced herself that Chemmy was as besotted as her other admirers and that it was only a matter of time before he legalized their relationship. The thought that he was now to marry some country nobody who, if Guy were to be believed, had more hair than wit, made her grind her teeth with jealousy and frustration.

"Well?" she demanded impatiently.

Guy looked up. "There is hope for you," he said. "Jennie don't want the Marquis. She thinks Chemmy's a fop and she's told him she wants a marriage of convenience and he's agreed to it.

34

It's up to us to see they keep it that way. Jennie's in love with me. It's up to you to keep Chemmy in love with you."

Alice's magnificent eyes gleamed with hope. Then she said softly, "And what do you want out of it, my so dear Mr. Chalmers?"

He looked at her thoughtfully. They were seated in her boudoir. She was wearing an elaborate silk and lace negligée which did little to conceal her charms. Her hair, emerging from under her pretty lace nightcap, spread over her shoulders in a golden haze.

"I want what Chemmy's been enjoying," he said finally. "Without payment."

"What?" she gasped. "How *dare* you! What kind of woman do you think I am?"

"A very desperate one," said Guy.

"I can give you money," she said.

"I'll do without that for once," laughed Guy. "Old Lord Bemyss and his lady can't last for much longer and they're not the type to leave their money to a girl so that leaves only me. I know Lord Charles has got it all salted away. He ought to have. Lives like a miser. No, it must be you, my dear, if you want my help."

Alice sighed and looked at him. Up till this morning's call, he had merely been one of the many admirers who formed her court. He was not ill-looking, in fact any woman not knowing the vicious side of his nature would consider him handsome, with his strong, straight figure and boyish good looks.

"What if Chemmy should find out?" she whispered.

"He won't, I promise you," said Guy, getting to his feet and crossing the little room to stand over her. "You bed with me and I'll ruin Miss Jennie Bemyss so badly that *no one* will want her."

"Very well," said Alice, moving to lead the way into the adjoining bedroom, but he forestalled her.

"No. Here," he commanded, taking her in his arms and pulling her down to the floor. "Here!"

That very afternoon, the Marquis of Charrington surveyed his mistress with something approaching pity. She looked tired, white, exhausted and ill. He thought of what Perry had said and realized his friend might have struck upon the truth. He had not expected Alice to take the news of his marriage so hard.

"I am truly sorry, Alice," he said gently. "I should have given you warning."

Alice remembered Guy's instructions and gave him a brave smile. "I cannot keep you, Chemmy," she said softly. "But remember, I shall love no one else and I shall always be here if you should want me."

I really have misjudged her, thought the Marquis with a stab of guilt. *I had thought she only cared for my money.*

"Come Alice," he said, kissing her gently. "We shall still be friends, shall we not? We have had many good times together and I do not wish us to part in sadness or in anger."

Alice smiled at him bravely. "I cannot pretend not to be sad . . . even for your sake," she said in a low voice. "But I, at least, will remain faithful to you."

"There is really no future for us," he said, dreading to hurt her but feeling he must do his duty. "This betrothal was arranged a long time ago. I did not mean to go through with it but I feel I must have an heir at some time."

"I could have given you an heir," she said, staring at her entwined fingers.

"You could equally have given Trace an heir . . . or Richards," said a nasty voice in Chemmy's brain but he remained silent.

Alice rose to her feet and rang the bell. It had been a truly horrid day and she suddenly wanted to be alone. The battle for Chemmy's heart should commence tomorrow. But not today. Dear God, not today! She was too tired and sore and humiliated to think.

The Marquis took his leave in a thoughtful frame of mind. For all he was sorry for Alice, he was puzzled by the peculiar atmosphere of the house. It almost seemed to *smell* of another man. He would not have been at all surprised to see someone else's hat and cane in the hallway. Then he gave himself a mental shake and walked briskly in the direction of his club. He was becoming as hypersensitive and moody as old Perry.

Chapter Three

"Is this the place?" demanded Perry, chewing nervously on the knob of his cane.

The Marquis took it to be a rhetorical question and did not trouble himself to answer.

Perry climbed nimbly down from the box of the carriage and stared in awe at Runbury Manor.

"Leafy, ain't it?" he exclaimed in awe. "I've never seen so much cursed ivy in my life. Never! Like living in a damned great tree. Are you sure there's brickwork under all that?"

"Yes," said the Marquis, climbing down to join him. "Lord Charles likes the ivy. He says it keeps out the drafts."

The Marquis and Perry had arrived on the day before the wedding to stay at Runbury Manor as houseguests.

He knocked loudly on the door. There was a long silence and then the slow shuffling sound of footsteps.

The door creaked open and Perry stared at the elderly footman in his ancient livery.

"It's like one of Mrs. Radcliffe's romances," he whispered to Chemmy as they followed the aged retainer across the dark hall. "Is it haunted?"

"Only by a pack of elderly dogs," smiled the Marquis.

They were ushered into the Blue Saloon.

"I shall inform my lord of your arrival," said the footman before creaking his way out.

Both friends stood and looked around them. The house was very quiet. The sunlight struggled through the ivy leaves and dirty glass to waver and dance on the spindly furniture and the army of whirring and ticking clocks. Several dogs snored and yelped in their sleep. A draft blew under the door and sent great tufts and balls of dog hair rolling gently about the room.

There was a sour smell of drains and dog. The Marquis struggled with the catch of one of the windows and succeeded in prying it open, letting in all the heavy, hot smells of summer to banish the older scents of the stuffy room.

"I shall catch the cholera or the typhoid," said Perry gloomily. "I only hope the maids of honor are pretty."

"It's a very quiet wedding," said the Marquis. "But for your sake, Perry, I hope there are some pretty faces around."

The Marquis dismissed two of the dogs from the chairs and motioned his friend to be seated.

Perry sat in his usual pose, right on the edge of his chair, and plugged his mouth with the knob of his cane.

The English countryside was enjoying a rare heatwave. Perry ran a finger along the inside of his cravat and wondered how his friend could look so cool.

The starch of his own cravat was losing a battle

with the heat and his leather breeches were beginning to feel as if they had mysteriously shrunk.

"It's not fair," he burst out, saying as usual what was uppermost in his mind. "We manage to stop powdering our hair because of the price of flour and then, just as we're getting comfortable again, Brummell invents the starched cravat, and there we are, cornflowered up to the ears! Don't the heat bother you?"

"It does," said the Marquis. "I would like a large cool bath . . . if they *have* baths in this establishment."

"I doubt it," said Perry gloomily. "What I want to know is . . . do *people* live here? I mean, is *anyone* going to come? The place is as quiet as a tomb and just about as busy."

As if in contradiction an explosion sounded from a distance, followed by a high feminine scream. Both men jumped to their feet and stared at each other. Then there was the sound of light, rapid footsteps and the double doors opened to reveal Lady Priscilla. Her cap was askew, her face flushed, and her dress was running with a nasty, sticky, brown stuff.

Perry thought for one awful moment that her ladyship had crawled out of the drains.

"My brandied peaches," she wailed. "Oh, it's the *heat.* They were fermenting nicely and then . . . *bang!* The whole jar exploded over me. And I did so want to have brandied peaches for the wedding breakfast."

The Marquis drew up a chair, decanting an old dog from it as he did so, and Lady Priscilla sank into it gratefully, dripping peach juice and brandy on the floor.

"May I present my friend, Mr. Peregrine Deighton," said the Marquis.

"No, you can't. Not now," said Lady Priscilla vaguely. "Have you seen Jennie? *She* will know what to do."

"I'm here, Grandmama," said a light voice from the doorway. Jennie Bemyss stood surveying them. Her black hair was tumbled on her shoulders and she wore an old and patched gown, but Perry was easily able to see why his friend had decided to honor the betrothal.

"Oh, Jennie," cried her ladyship. "It is the peaches, you know. They exploded, just like that, and now we shall have none for your wedding."

"We shall have fresh strawberries instead," said Jennie comfortingly.

"But *fresh* fruit is so uninteresting," exclaimed Lady Priscilla. Then her face brightened. "I know. I shall soak them in Kirsch. Now, I wonder if we have enough fresh cream? No matter. I shall make mock cream. Do you know," she demanded earnestly of Perry, "how to make mock cream?"

"No," said Perry, looking at her uneasily.

" 'Tis quite simple. You just beat a fresh egg in a basin and slowly pour boiling tea over it. Believe me, no one will ever know the difference."

"I think I might," said Perry, ever honest.

"*Do* you?" queried Lady Priscilla, much interested. "I shall give you a test. It will only take me a minute to make some. I believe Martha . . . our cook, you know . . . has some old tea left over from yesterday. I *never* throw anything away."

"Please . . . oh, please don't," gabbled Perry wildly. "I mean, it will be too much effort."

"Not at all," smiled Lady Priscilla, rising to her feet.

"Oh, *no!*" cried poor Perry, quite overset. "*I don't want any.*"

"Then don't have any! There!" said Lady Priscilla with sudden petulance. "Who *are* these gentlemen, Jennie?"

Jennie solemnly made the introductions, re-introducing the Marquis and adding, with a sympathetic look at Perry, that she was sure the gentlemen would wish to retire to their rooms and change after their journey.

To their surprise, it was Jennie herself who led the way up the broad worm-eaten steps of the staircase.

"Don't you have a housekeeper?" asked Perry as he followed Jennie along a bewildering chain of dark corridors.

"Alas, no," said Jennie. "Poor Mrs. Briggs died last month. It took us some time to realize she was dead, you know. She was very old and did not move about much. Ah, here are *your* rooms, Mr. Deighton. She pushed open a heavy door and then turned to the Marquis. "And now if you will follow me, my lord . . ."

"My friends call me Chemmy," said the Marquis, bending his head as the corridor roof suddenly seemed to take a downward plunge. Jennie did not answer but led him down a little flight of steps and then pushed open a door. "I hope you will find this comfortable enough."

"I'm sure I shall manage," said Chemmy looking around the sparsely furnished room. "Jennie, I . . ."

But his young fiancée had already dropped him a demure curtsey and closed the door behind her.

The Marquis crossed to the windows and eventually managed to open them. The view was mostly obscured by ivy. He suddenly felt dirty and tired, and pulled on the bellrope.

He waited a considerable length of time until he heard the door opening behind him. Without turning around, he snapped, "Well, you took your time about it, laddie. Fetch me a bath directly!"

"That is a little difficult," said the voice of his fiancée.

"Goodness!" said the Marquis, swinging around. "Have you *no* servants?"

"Indeed we do," said Jennie earnestly. "But they are not in the way of dealing with houseguests. They are all very old, you see, and when they die, my grandfather does not replace them. I carry up my own bath water. Don't you have a valet?"

"He is traveling here separately," said the Marquis. "Is there a pump?"

"Oh, yes, behind the stables."

"Very well," said the Marquis. "I shall go and put my head under it before dinner. You *do* have dinner?"

"At four o'clock every afternoon."

"That leaves me an hour to wrestle with the pump," said the Marquis.

A faint rattle of carriage wheels sounded through the open window.

"Guy!" cried Jennie, her face lighting up with delight. She flew from the room, banging the door noisily behind her.

"I wonder," said the Marquis to himself as he stared thoughtfully at the closed door, "I wonder if I should go through with this."

But no sign of his doubts appeared on his handsome face at the dinner table. He was groomed and polished and scented, magnificent in silk coat and knee breeches. Jewels glittered in his cravat and on his long white fingers. As they sat down to dinner, he raised his quizzing glass and indolently surveyed his fiancée.

Jennie blushed to the roots of her tangled hair. She had not even bothered to change her dress for dinner, hoping thereby to show the Marquis how little she cared for him, but the plan had somehow backfired. The elegant Marquis, without moving a muscle or opening his mouth made her feel like a scrubby hoyden.

Guy may have convinced her that the Marquis

was an effete dandy, but she could not help feeling that the elegantly arrayed Marquis was paying a courteous compliment to his hosts by his formal dress and wished that Guy had done the same, instead of having his shirt open at the neck and a Belcher handkerchief tied around his throat.

Perry was in a thoroughly bad mood. He had had a long and exhausting fight with an elderly hound who had taken possession of his bed, and the hound had won the battle, depriving Perry of a much needed afternoon's sleep. He had tugged on the bell cord until it had come away in his hand but no one had answered his summons. The copper water cans on the marble washstand were empty of everything, save dust.

Now, the cooked remains of a tough and athletic cow stared up at him from his dinner plate. The meal had begun with a mulligatawny soup that defied description. This had been followed by a dry and withered salmon at one end of the table and a greasy and oily turbot, flanked by bony and brittle smelts, at the other.

The muscular beef fought back gamely as he tried to cut it into small pieces, since fashion decreed that he must spear a piece of everything on his plate on his fork at the same time and pop the whole of this compound cookery between his jaws. He was further frustrated by a large helping of peas, which he was expected to eat with an old-fashioned, two-pronged fork. The heat of the room was oppressive and the smell from the side dishes, which appeared to be several abortive attempts at Continental cooking, made him feel queasy.

He gave up the battle and toyed moodily with his wine glass, watching Jennie's animated face as she laughed at something that Guy was saying. He then turned his gaze to his friend. Could not the Marquis *see* that the ill-garbed, ill-behaved hoyden was besotted with young Guy?

The elderly footman fuddled the remains of the beef to the sideboard and then carried forward a ham, a fowl and a tongue with frail, trembling arms. What had happened to the butler? Chemmy could have told him that the butler had probably died but Chemmy was keeping up an easy flow of conversation, not one whit abashed by the awful food, the strange company or the heat.

At last the dreadful meal was over. Lady Priscilla led Jennie off to the drawing room and Lord Charles (as was the custom), led the gentlemen into the garden to urinate on the lawn.

Guy had drawn Lord Charles a little way across the lawn from the others but his voice carried on the still night air. "Saw a prime elegant tit at Tatersall's, sir," Guy was saying. "It's going for fifty guineas . . . lovely bit of horseflesh, as fine a bit of blood as you ever saw."

"Ah," sighed Lord Charles reminiscently, "that reminds me of my old mare, Clara. What a stout heart that poor beast had. Never a nag to touch her on the field. Ah, Clara!"

"As I was saying," went on Guy with a slight

edge to his voice. "It's a matter of fifty guineas."

"What's that?"

"*Fifty guineas,* sir."

"Very, very, very kind of you, dear boy. But keep your money. Keep it, dear boy. We are in funds at the moment. Yes, yes, yes. But very kind. Yes, *very* kind . . ." He ambled towards the Marquis and Perry, while Guy closed his mouth which had fallen open in surprise. Either Lord Charles was senile or cunning, and Guy thought rather grimly that it was the latter.

Lord Charles led the gentlemen into the drawing room. Jennie had changed her dress and combed her hair and was sitting, engaged in placing delicate little stitches on a piece of tapestry.

The Marquis made his way towards Jennie, who immediately arose and crossed to the pianoforte which she proceeded to play with more enthusiasm than finesse until it was time for the company to retire to bed, being all of eight o'clock in the evening — a time when the Marquis and Mr. Deighton were usually sitting down to dinner.

In response to his friend's pleas, the Marquis removed the hound from Perry's bed before retiring to his own.

He thought of how pretty Jennie had looked that evening and decided that it was just as well they were getting married after all.

Unlike most brides, Jennie, as she walked up

the aisle on her grandfather's arm the next day, searched her groom's face hopefully for some sign of anger. But to her disappointment, he seemed as bland and smiling as ever.

She had secretly hoped that the sight of her wedding dress would have made him call off the marriage. Now he did not seem to notice or care and she was left feeling like a quiz, having to endure the shocked stare of the best man.

Perry could hardly believe his eyes. He did not know that Jennie was wearing Lady Priscilla's wedding gown. He only saw that she was dressed in yellow, dingy lace, heavily embroidered with pearls, which kept escaping from their moorings and rattling off into the pews.

He felt he owed it to his friend to stop this disastrous marriage and, in a last ditch attempt, pretended he had forgotten the ring. The Marquis merely smiled, drew his own ring from his finger and fitted it over Jennie's smaller one.

Only after the happy couple had signed the register in the vestry of the little Norman church and were moving slowly down the aisle did Perry become aware of impending doom.

Standing at the entrance to the church, dressed in the very latest of Parisian modes and surrounded by a group of fashionable friends, stood Alice Waring.

Jennie noticed that one of the most beautiful women she had ever seen was staring at her gown with amused contempt. The Marquis halted in front of Alice and presented his bride. Awed by the fashionable dress of Alice and her friends, Jennie dropped an awkward curtsey. Immediately several hundred pearls broke from the worn threads of her gown and rattled noisily to the ground.

Alice gave an enchanting laugh and her eyes caressed the Marquis. "Dear me, Chemmy," she drawled, "you should send your little bride to join Wellington's artillery. Those Frenchies would soon be routed."

Then she bit her lip in vexation. The Marquis was looking at her with a rather hard gleam in his eyes and she knew she had gone too far.

"You must forgive us for not inviting you to the wedding breakfast, Mrs. Waring," said the Marquis gently. "But it is, as you see, a family party. Come, my dear."

Jennie gratefully allowed her husband to lead her away from the mocking eyes of the watching group.

She was now desperate to return to the Manor and change her dress, and, after she had done that, enjoy all the luxury of a good cry.

But on descending the stairs to join the wedding breakfast, she found the Marquis making his apologies to his hosts and their various guests. He was anxious to take his bride directly to London, he said, turning and giving Jennie a warm smile and ignoring the mutinous look on her face. Perry had fallen into the clutches of the burly maid of honor, Sally Byles, Jennie's only friend, who lived in the next county, and was hoping that Chemmy would take him, too.

But the efficient Marquis had had his bride's trunks corded up and placed in the back of the phaeton and was now gently urging her towards the door.

Jennie waved a tearful farewell — more to Guy who was standing outside on the steps watching her with amusement — rather than to her old home.

The carriage rattled briskly down the drive and past the untenanted lodge with Jennie perched beside her new husband and John, the groom, clinging on the back.

After several miles, Jennie found her voice.

"Is this how we are to go on, sir?" she gritted. "Are *my* wishes never to be consulted? For your information, my grandmother expected us to stay for a few days." Her lip trembled. "But now it seems that no sooner is the ring on my finger than I am to be wrenched from my beloved home."

The Marquis reined in his horses and looked down at his furious bride. "My heart of hearts!" he exclaimed, "How could I be so callous? To think that . . . following my own selfish whim, of course . . . I had planned to take you to my box at the opera and then to the fireworks display at Vauxhall afterward. I was even silly enough to have the family diamonds cleaned for you to wear! But you have a mind above such flummery. Of course, I will take you back to your beloved home directly." He ignored a low groan from his groom and edged the carriage around in the narrow country road and proceeded to set a brisk pace back towards the Manor.

Jennie bit her lip and did not know whether to throw a temper tantrum, box his ears or burst into tears. She contented herself by muttering a stifled, "Thank you." She tried unsuccessfully to fight away the vision of herself, bedecked in diamonds, sitting at the opera, enjoying the music and all her new-found position in society as a wealthy young marchioness.

The guests gave them a noisy welcome, with the exception of Guy who had left for London.

The wedding breakfast was turning out a resounding success, much to Perry's surprise. The ancient cook, Martha, had succumbed to a bottle of gin and had been unable to cook anything. But the ladies of the county had not yet learned the fine art of allowing servants to do absolutely everything and had been trained, in the old way of the last century, to do everything a servant could, and better. They accordingly had donned pinafores over their gowns descended en masse to the ancient kitchens and had proceeded to compete with each other in producing the most delightful delicacies.

Perry had reached the bottom of his first bottle of port and was thinking dreamily that Sally Byles was not a burly, masculine girl after all. She was merely suffering from an excess of puppy fat and the buoyancy of seventeen summers and when she, too, took her turn in the kitchen and emerged floury and triumphant, bearing a plate of delicious apricot tartlets, his admiration knew no bounds. He begged her to join him, noticing for the first time that her eyes were a pretty periwinkle blue and that her mouth was small enough to please the highest stickler of the *ton*.

Sally was only too delighted to gain the attention of this dapper, older man. She complimented him on his friend the Marquis' elegance and said that Jennie was indeed a lucky girl.

"I hope she appreciates him, that's all," said Perry, broaching his second bottle.

Sally's blue eyes opened to their widest. "I haven't seen much of Jennie recently," said Sally. "We live so far apart. But I feel sure Jennie must be in love. She is not the kind of girl to marry for money."

"Oh, no?" said the indiscreet Perry gloomily.

"No!" said Sally flying to quick defense of her friend. "And his lordship will find he has a treasure for his wife. Jennie is worth a hundred beautiful women . . . even as beautiful as that gorgeous creature I saw in church. Who is she?"

And Perry, fuddled with wine and fatigue, and plagued with his customary honesty, said baldly, "That is Mrs. Alice Waring, Chemmy's mistress."

Sally stared at him, puzzled and alarmed, and began to edge away, wishing to retreat to her safe world where young girls got married and lived happily ever after. She looked across to where Jennie was standing, talking to one of the wedding guests. She looked very young and vulnerable. "I shall tell her," said Sally.

Shock sobered Perry. "Oh, my cursed tongue," he cried. "Please forget what I said, Miss Byles. That affair is most definitely over. Why, anyone can see that Chemmy is in love with his wife!"

Sally stared at the Marquis, who smiled lazily back. There was no emotion registered on his face other than a rather sleepy good humor.

"And what do you expect Jennie to *do* about it?" pressed Perry desperately. "Come now, Miss Byles, you must promise me you will not say a word about it."

"I don't know," said Sally mulishly. "I shall say nothing at the moment. But I am to go with my parents to London next month and if I see any sign that the Marquis has not terminated the liaison, then I shall tell Jennie. So there!" And with that Perry had to be content. He returned to his bottle for solace and wondered what on earth had caused the couple to return to the Manor.

Jennie was wondering if she had gone mad. She had suddenly remembered that Lady Priscilla had roused herself from her customary vague indifference to have a bridal suite prepared. The light was fading outside and the guests' jokes were becoming bawdier and several were wondering noisily why the couple did not go to bed.

At last she felt a hand on her arm and found her large husband smiling down at her. "Come,

Jennie," he said. "It is time to retire."

The noisy guests cheered them up the stairs, blowing hunting horns and hallooing and whooping.

Feeling as if she were walking in a dream, Jennie allowed Chemmy to lead her up the stairs and along the twisting corridors to the bridal chamber. She did wonder, however, how her lord knew where it was.

The old four-poster bed had been turned back to reveal damp and yellowing sheets, which smelled strongly of camphor. The Marquis crossed and opened the window and was immediately greeted with cheers, whoops and advice from the garden below. He waved his hand good-naturedly to the guests and turned to his bride.

"I shall use the dressing room," he said. "You may prepare for bed here."

"Are you going to sleep with me?" squeaked Jennie in alarm.

"Yes," he said good-humoredly. "I am going to sleep with you. Beside you, that is. Come now. You do not expect me to sleep on the floor."

"I could go to my old room," whispered Jennie.

"So you could," he agreed, "but our guests would certainly find out, since I believe your room has been given up to one of them. Be a good child and get into bed and go to sleep. I am not going to touch you."

He strode off into the dressing room, leaving Jennie standing beside the bed.

Jennie scrambled hastily out of her clothes and then into an old flannel nightdress, which she buttoned tight up to the neck despite the close heat of the room.

"I could have spared myself this if we had gone to London," she thought bitterly. "Oh, Guy, where are you?"

She lay rigidly on the bed, staring sightlessly up at the canopy. She did not believe for one minute that the Marquis would simply go to sleep. He would make love to her, of that she was sure, and then she would really be his wife. Perhaps he would make her fall in love with him and then she need no longer feel so guilty about being married to one man and being in love with another. Perhaps it would not be so bad after all.

The dressing room door opened.

"What are you wearing?" screeched Jennie, suddenly sitting bolt upright.

"Nothing," said her husband's amused voice. "I am in my buffs, my dear. It is the way I usually sleep."

Jennie sank down into the bed, pulled the covers up to her throat and screwed her eyes shut. The bed gave a protesting creak as her husband's great bulk climbed in beside her.

"Good night, my wife," he said softly.

But Jennie did not answer. She kept her body rigid and her eyes shut tight and then started counting under her breath. When she had reached two hundred, she slowly opened her eyes. The merrymaking of the guests sounded noisily from the garden and, beside her, came the faint gentle sounds of rythmical breathing.

She cautiously propped herself up on one elbow. In the faint light of the moon shining in at the window, it was all too clear to Jennie that her lord had fallen fast asleep.

It was then she began to shake with muddled distress and anger. Her looking glass told her that she was pretty. But obviously her husband did not think so.

One of the wedding guests had decided to serenade the bridal couple, and his pleasant tenor voice floated in through the window on the still summer air. It was a familiar Scotch ballad made famous by Mrs. Mountain, who had sung it at Vauxhall. The sweet, lilting notes echoed in Jennie's ears like a dirge.

> Kirkcaldy is a bonny place,
> And Jemmy lives beside it;
> 'Twas there we saw each other's face
> Whatever may betide it:
> But be it ill, or be it not,
> I dinna care a feather;
> For soon at Kirk we'll tie the knot,
> And we shall live together!
> O! we shall live together, laddie,
> We shall live together.

"Yes, we shall live together," murmured poor Jennie. "But oh! How far apart!"

Chapter Four

Runbury Manor basked in the lazy heat of yet another perfect summer day. The birds twittered briefly in the ivy as the sun rose, falling silent as the heat burned the dew from the shaggy lawns and lowered another few inches in the lake.

Jennie awoke late, already feeling hot and gritty. She was alone in the great bed. She climbed out and washed and dressed hurriedly, lest her lord should suddenly appear.

But the great house seemed imprisoned in hot silence. She made her way downstairs, looking at her home, it seemed to her, for the first time.

There was no denying that it stank abominably. The great hall door stood open but no fresh air blew in to relieve the heavy, musty air. Dust motes danced lazily in shafts of sunlight, which struck through the leaded pains of the windows to mercilessly highlight the worn, spindly furniture and threadbare rugs.

Jennie ate her breakfast in solitary grandeur and then, becoming impatient, went in search of another human being.

Lady Priscilla was seated in the morning room, carefully studying a letter with a large magnifying glass.

She looked up as her granddaughter appeared

and gave Jennie a fond, vague smile.

"So kind," she said fluttering the letter. "You are indeed a lucky young lady to have such an understanding husband."

"Why is he writing a letter to you?" asked Jennie, puzzled.

"Read it my dear. 'Tis all that is charming!"

"You know I cannot read," said Jennie, crossly. "I have been taught to sign my name. If you will remember, grandfather insisted that that was all I needed to know."

"He did?" Lady Priscilla picked up the parchment from her lap and proceeded to read, unaware of the conflict of emotions on her granddaughter's face.

" 'Dear Lady Priscilla,' " she read, " 'I am making an early departure for London and wish you to make my farewells to my bride. Although the Season is over, I have a depressing round of social commitments . . . balls, parties, breakfasts and masquerades. Jennie is very young and *very* attached to her home and I feel it would be unfair of me to subject her to such a boring round of social duties so soon. Perhaps when she is a little older, she will learn to endure them as I do. For the moment, I feel I should be a monster, indeed, to take such a young girl away from all she loves. Yr. humble and obedient servant, Cyril, Marquis of Charrington.' Now isn't that thoughtful!" cried Lady Priscilla, dropping the letter.

"He knows you are little more than a child.

Most husbands would not be so considerate. What a gentleman!"

"Yes, Grandmama," said Jennie in a stifled voice and then she fairly ran from the room and out into the garden.

She thought of London, she thought of all the balls and parties she was missing, and groaned aloud. Why hadn't she gone with him the night before?

She must try somehow to write to him. She could print a few simple words and at least she knew her alphabet. She remembered having seen a copy of Dr. Johnson's dictionary somewhere in the library. Perhaps with the help of that she could compose a letter.

Jennie did not consider that she could have ridden to Sally Byles' home and asked that young lady for assistance for Jennie believed her friend to be as unlettered as herself, Guy sharing her grandfather's views that an uneducated lady was a true gentlewoman.

She entered the silence of the house again and went into the library. Everything was unnaturally quiet and still, the last of the wedding guests having set out very early in the morning.

But search as she might, Jennie could not find the dictionary. In desperation she pulled open the double doors of a cupboard in the corner and then reeled back as a mountain of newsprint came tumbling about her ears.

Lord Charles was forever ripping and cutting pieces out of the morning paper. Jennie had often wondered what had happened to them since nothing at the Manor was ever thrown away. Well, now she knew!

She sat down under the mountain of fluttering newspaper and cried and cried with rage at the stupid Marquis, who had left her in this stupid house and all through her own stupid fault.

After a time, she dried her eyes. At least there was one bright spot on the horizon of her gloomy mind. Guy would surely come to see her. She was no longer a young miss but a married woman. She now belonged to that mysterious society who were able to have all these delicious liaisons without anyone censuring them.

All she had to do was wait for Guy to arrive, which he surely would the minute he found out she was not in London.

But the long hot days stretched endlessly. The sun rose and set in a cloudless sky. The lawns turned brown and gold and the dusty gold and brown leaves began to turn and whisper along the weedy drive and nobody came. No Guy, no husband.

Like a sleeping beauty trapped in some particularly noisome castle, Jennie drifted through the days as she had always done and sometimes, during the long, hot, sleepless nights, she wondered if her marriage had been all a dream.

As the incredible un-English summer blazed on into a red and gold autumn, Guy Chalmers stalked away from the Marquis' town residence in Albemarle Street with the butler's now familiar message ringing in his ears, "No, sir, I regret that my lord and my lady are not yet returned from the country."

Guy racked his brains. He had not thought the Marquis would have taken Jennie straight to his country estate. He had suggested to the Marquis' frosty-faced butler that he, Guy, might pay the newly wedded couple a visit, but this had been received with the stern rejoinder of, "No, sir, that is not possible. His lordship definitely said that he did not wish visitors."

Alice Waring had grown increasingly distant and had taken to mocking Guy and calling him a failure. He had been unable to repeat his delicious experience in her boudoir. Alice claimed coldly that Guy was ineffectual and would be unable to do anything to come between the married couple.

The Marquis' estates lay in Kent, a good two days' ride from London, reflected Guy. He *must* do something. There was, after all, a faint possibility that Lord Charles might leave Jennie some of his money. But a ruined Jennie would not inherit a penny and Guy would undoubtedly get it all. With money and Jennie ruined, he could enjoy the grateful Alice's favors any time he wished, having enjoyed Jennie's in the ruining process.

It was then that he hit on an idea. He would ride to Kent and call at the Marquis' home claiming that his horse had shed a shoe. He would say that he was on his road to Dover to visit friends. That way he could see Jennie and ascertain whether the marriage of convenience still existed.

Alice had refused to discuss her liaison with the Marquis and so Guy had come to believe that the Marquis had merely set Alice up as mistress in order to follow the fashion, without indulging in the pleasures of the bed. A man so wed to his tailor could have little time for women!

Two days hard riding through the hot sun-baked countryside brought him to the gates of Charrington Court.

He drew his horse into the shelter of a high hedge and pried off one of its shoes. Then, leading it by the reins, he walked to the lodge gates.

A crusty and suspicious lodge keeper let him through, only after much exhaustive questioning.

It was a long, long road to the Court from the gates. It seemed to wind through acres and acres of fields, then through a deer park, then through spacious formal gardens and then to the house itself, which was a great imposing early Georgian pile with two huge wings springing out from a central portico.

Guy was left kicking his heels for some time before he was finally conducted up the stairs to his lordship's private sitting room.

The Marquis was sitting at his dressing table, wrapped in a magnificent brocade dressing gown and cleaning his nails with the single-minded absorption of a well-trained house cat. He was scented and barbered and appeared his usual elegant self, even in his present state of undress.

Guy did not know that the Marquis had only that morning taken off his dusty gaiters and sweaty clothes after helping with the last of the work of a bumper harvest. He only thought that he looked the perfect picture of the effete and bloodless aristocrat and put the breadth of his shoulder down to buckram wadding.

He told his carefully rehearsed story of his horse casting a shoe and the Marquis merely smiled at him sleepily, rang the bell, ordered a servant to tell the estate blacksmith to see to Mr. Chalmers' horse immediately and then turned his attention once more to his nails.

"I am looking forward to seeing Jennie, again," said Guy, breaking the silence at last.

So am I, thought the Marquis to himself, but he said instead, in a vague kind of way, "Ah, my wife? Yes, she seems to prefer the country to the social round of London."

"Where is she?" demanded Guy abruptly.

"Oh, somewhere about the countryside," said the Marquis, still in that maddeningly vague way.

"I shall be disappointed an' I do not see her," said Guy.

"Will you? How touching are these family ties," said the Marquis, examining an orange stick. "Well, you shall no doubt see her in London. We shall be returning there for the

Little Season. She will be desolated to have missed you."

"I could put off my visit to these people in Dover," said Guy desperately.

The Marquis got lazily to his feet and flung an arm around Guy's shoulders and gave him an affectionate hug.

"I wouldn't hear of it," he said, "but what a splendid chap you are to suggest it. But . . . alas! We of the social world must honor our commitments and I am sure you would rather be with your friends than play gooseberry here."

"I assure you, sir," said Guy stiffly, "that my friendship for Jennie is very close and very deep. She is my sole concern. She . . ."

"Then how relieved you must feel to know that she is safely married and has a husband to take all these nasty little worries from your shoulders," said the Marquis. "Ah, Dobbins, Mr. Chalmers' horse is ready? Splendid! Good day to you, Mr. Chalmers. We look forward to seeing you in town."

There was nothing for Guy to do but take his leave.

For the rest of the day, he travelled around the marches of the Marquis' vast estate, hoping for a glimpse of Jennie. But the countryside lay calm and smiling and empty under the hot sun.

Made desperate by fatigue, he returned to the lodge and rang the bell. This time there was no reply and the gates remained firmly closed. He could see the lodge keeper sitting by the open window in his shirt sleeves, smoking a clay pipe, but although he rang and shouted, the old man appeared to have gone unaccountably deaf.

After dark, he tried leading his horse through a break in the hedge and found himself looking down the long barrel of a gamekeeper's gun and it took a score of lies and apologies to extricate himself.

He then rode wearily to the local inn to be told by a surly landlord that there was no room. He asked for ale, and was told there was nothing to drink, and tired and intimidated by the sullen stares of the local yokels in the tap, he took himself off.

"What is the name of this cursed hostelry?" he asked himself, as he mounted his weary horse. He glanced up. The sign said, "The Marquis of Charrington" and Chemmy's painted, bland and amiable features stared down at him.

"Damn him!" thought Guy. "He saw through my story and is making sure I do not get near Jennie. Mayhap Alice will have some suggestion."

By the time he returned to London, two days later, he was in time to be informed that Mrs. Waring had left for the opera.

He hurried to his lodgings to change into his evening coat and knee breeches and managed to reach the Haymarket Theater by the first interval.

He went straight to Mrs. Waring's box, ignoring in his hurry the gentleman seated next to her, and demanded a few words with her in private.

Alice's eyes glowed with triumph and malice. "Certainly not!" she said. "Darling, tell this . . . person . . . to go away."

Guy looked at her companion and found himself staring into the thin, painted, malicious features of the Earl of Freize.

"Take yourself off," said the Earl, turning his gaze away from Guy. "You bore the lady."

"Mrs. Waring and I are *intimate* friends," grated Guy.

The Earl raised one finger. "Get rid of it," he said.

Two burly footmen appeared from the shadows at the back of the box.

Taken by surprise, Guy had no time to fight back. He was carried down the stairs like a sack of potatoes and out into the street, where he was dropped face down in the filth of the kennel in the middle of the road.

He staggered to his feet consumed with hate. Hate for the Marquis, hate for Alice who had so quickly found herself a new protector. And what did they have that he did not? Money. Money, and therefore, power.

There was nothing he could do now but wait for Jennie's return. By ruining Jennie he would cut her off from her grandparents and bring that smiling idiot of a Marquis to his knees.

After he had bathed and changed, he joined his cronies at Tothill and spent a splendid night roaming the streets with them, frightening and humiliating the weak and helpless. When a sultry dawn came up over London, he had boxed several Charlies, rolled several old people in the mud and had raped a serving girl on her way home. His *amour propre* was restored. He felt powerful again.

All he had to do was wait. . . .

Chapter Five

The Marquis rustled impatiently through his correspondence while a footman moved quietly about the room lighting candles, although it was only midday.

His lordship and a deluge of typically English weather had arrived back in London together. Rain thudded down on the roof and chuckled in the gutters. Rain streamed in waterfalls down the plate glass of the windows beyond which Albemarle Street wavered and danced as if all its gray buildings had found themselves at the bottom of the Thames.

"I would have thought she would have given up by now," said the Marquis to himself. "Perhaps she really does love that horrible home of hers after all," and then out loud, "What is it, Dobbins?"

"A Mr. Guy Chalmers has called."

"Tell Mr. Chalmers that my lord and my lady are not yet returned from the country," said the Marquis and then muttered, "Persistent beast!" after the footman had gone.

He started to sharpen a quill and prepared to deal with his correspondence, vowing for the umpteenth time to hire himself a secretary.

Once more he was interrupted by the entrance of the footman.

"Excuse me, my lord," said Dobbins, looking very worried, "but there is a young lady in the hall who says she is the Marchioness of Charrington."

A slow smile curved the Marquis' lips. "I'm very sure it is, Dobbins. Show her in!"

He got to his feet and turned around. A small bedraggled figure, clutching a bandbox, stood in the doorway.

It was indeed Jennie. She was wearing a white dimity dress which was miles too short, a bedraggled straw hat with two dripping feathers and a much-worn pelisse. She was clutching a bandbox in one hand and the remains of a parasol in the other.

She looked around in awe at the stately drawing room with its silk-paneled walls, elegant furniture and Chinese rugs, and at the apple wood fire crackling on the hearth. Finally she turned her eyes to her husband, taking in the exquisite cut of his coat of Bath Superfine, dove gray pantaloons and gleaming boots.

"I came," she said defiantly.

"So I see," remarked her husband pleasantly, "and I am very flattered that you have managed to tear yourself away from the pastoral joys of your home."

"I felt my duty was to be with my husband," said Jennie stiffly.

"Very proper," said the Marquis. "Before we

continue our conversation, I will get the house-keeper to show you to your rooms. We will talk further after you have changed."

"I want to talk *now!*" said Jennie, stamping her foot.

"Later," he said gently, as the housekeeper rustled into the room. "Mrs. Benton. Take her ladyship to her rooms and make sure that all that is necessary is done for her."

Mrs. Benton, an awe-inspiring figure in black bombazine, majestically led the way and Jennie meekly followed, little rivulets of water running from her sodden clothes.

It had been another hot, humid, sunny day when she had escaped from her home. Her previous pleas that she be allowed to join her husband had been met by shocked opposition from both her grandparents. It was her duty to wait quietly at home until her husband sent for her, they had said.

Jennie had begun to burn with a steady fury against the absent Marquis, whom she imagined dancing and partying from dawn to dusk.

She had bought herself an outside seat on the coach after walking several weary miles to the crossroads.

As the coach had clattered down the long hill towards London, the purple clouds which had been massing all afternoon suddenly burst. She had been soaked to the skin by the time the coach had set her down at her destination and then the hack, which she had hired to take her to

Albemarle Street, had dropped her at the wrong address. By the time she had found the Marquis' home, she had felt she would never be dry again.

She became aware that Mrs. Benton was pushing open a mahogany door and Jennie blinked at the splendor of the rooms in front of her. An exquisite little sitting room decorated in rose and gold led into a spacious bedroom, with a great Chinese lacquered bed.

Mrs. Benton looked at her doubtfully. "Have you your lady's maid with you, my lady?" she asked.

"No," said Jennie, biting her lip. "She . . . er . . . preferred to stay in the country. She is very old." This was somewhat the truth since the lady's maid that Jennie had shared with her grand-mother had died two years ago and would have been in the region of ninety had she lived. "I shall manage for the present," said Jennie, trying to adopt a haughty manner and failing miser-ably.

"Then I shall send two footmen up with your bath," said Mrs. Benton. "As my lord probably informed you, you will find your new wardrobe in the little dressing room over there. If you need anything further, my lady, please ring. I shall call to conduct you to my lord in an hour."

Jennie waited impatiently until Mrs. Benton had curtsied herself out and then flew to the dressing room, which was off the bedroom.

She opened the doors of the closets and stared, wide-eyed.

There were morning dresses, opera gowns, ball gowns, carriage dresses and walking costumes — a whole treasure trove of silk and lace and muslin met her startled eyes. She slowly slid open the long drawers of a low boy and found them brim full of lace and silk underthings. In the top drawers were gloves and fans. A stack of hat boxes stood in one corner and rows of dainty shoes, slippers and boots stood neatly arranged at the foot of the closet.

How had he known her size so exactly? Why had he not written asking her to come — since he had gone to all this trouble?

But Jennie was too young and feminine to worry too much. And too excited over so many new and beautiful things. She thought of Guy's handsome face lighting up in surprise as he saw the transformation.

She bathed thoroughly, relishing the luxury of not having to carry away the dirty bath water herself.

With fingers that trembled slightly, she pulled a few of the lacy undergarments from the drawers and then searched along the row of dresses.

She finally chose a silk plaid dress with a high lace collar and long tight sleeves trimmed with lace at the cuffs. She then sat down at the dressing table and tried to twist her curls into some semblance of a fashionable hairstyle.

When Mrs. Benton escorted her down the stairs again, Jennie was conscious of a rising sense of excitement. What would her husband say when he saw how pretty she looked?

The Marquis was already seated at the luncheon table when Jennie was ushered in. He gave her a welcoming smile but, to Jennie's disappointment, made no comment on her transformation.

"Sit down my dear," he said, "and tell me your news. I have missed you."

"Then why did you leave me at home?" demanded Jennie sulkily, shaking out her napkin.

The Marquis looked shocked. "Me? Take you away from your beloved home? No, my heart, I left that decision entirely to you. Do your grandparents know where you are?"

"I wrote them a real letter," said Jennie proudly.

"A *real* letter," said the Marquis, much amused. "What, then, is an unreal letter?"

Jennie gave him a sullen look and flushed to the roots of her hair. How could she tell him of the hours she had labored over the dictionary or, in fact, of the hours she had taken to find that elusive book.

"We are invited to the Devey's ball tonight," said the Marquis. "Would you care to go?"

"Oh, yes," breathed Jennie, her sullen expression vanishing to be replaced by one of delight.

"Then I suggest after you have finished your lunch, you lie down for the afternoon and rest. I shall choose something for you to wear."

"You'll *what?*" said Jennie, dropping her fork.

"I would have you know, my lord, that I am perfectly capable of choosing my own gown."

"You will be, very soon," he said calmly. "But for the moment you will be guided by me."

"Either I choose my own gown," said Jennie, very slowly and distinctly, "or I do not go."

"As you will," replied her lord with great good humor.

"You are infuriating," hissed Jennie. "I mean to go to that ball and I mean to go in a gown of my own choosing. Either you agree to it or I shall . . . I shall . . . I shall hold my breath."

"No, I won't agree," said the Marquis, equably.

"Then I shall hold my breath and if you do not agree to let me have my way, I shall *die!*"

She took a deep breath and screwed up her eyes. The Marquis sat back in his chair and surveyed her with interest.

Jennie waited in agony for him to give in and at least try to coax and cajole her. The delicious smell of the food on her plate was making her feel weak with hunger. She had never smelled such delicious food before.

Tears of frustration began to gather in the corner of her eyes and the Marquis took pity on her.

He moved around the table in a leisurely way and gave her a resounding slap on the back.

She gasped and choked and glared at him like an angry kitten. "I shall let you have your way this time," she muttered. "But it is dangerous to cross me, my lord." She looked across the table at him. He had returned to his seat and was holding his napkin up to his face. His eyes were as tearful as Jennie's and she realized he was trying not to laugh out loud.

She looked at him angrily from under the spikes of her eyelashes and then said reluctantly, "Oh, very well. Just this time."

"Come, my dear," smiled the Marquis. "Tell me you are at least pleased with your new clothes."

Jennie had the grace to blush. She should have thanked him immediately. "I am v-very g-grateful for all the beautiful gowns," she muttered in a voice which sounded to her own ears very ungracious.

"It is my pleasure to give you gifts. Not every husband is blessed with so elegant a wife," he said, leaning back in his chair and watching her with lazy amusement. "Now, tell me, how was your summer?"

"Oh, it was vastly amusing," cried Jennie, rallying quickly. Not for one minute would she let this enigmatic husband of hers know of the long days of boredom. "We had a few parties and balls in the county, so the days passed very well."

"Indeed," he smiled. "You must have been very sad to leave it all. Why did you leave your grandparents a letter and then endure such a tedious journey? You should have written to me and I would have made all the arrangements for your journey to town."

He studied the top of his wife's dark curls as she bent her head suddenly over her plate. "They said I should wait until you sent for me," she said at last. She looked up quickly but his face betrayed nothing more than amiable interest. "I acted on an impulse."

"I am flattered," he said. "It must have been frightful traveling in the storm. You did not take the stage, I trust."

"Oh, but I did!" said Jennie, "and I rode outside." Forgetting her defiant role, she began to describe the journey, the discomfort of the stage, gaily mimicking the voices of the other passengers, so engrossed in her story that she failed to notice the dawning look of admiration on her husband's face.

"There is no need to go through such an experience again," he said quietly. "I am here to look after you, you know . . . although at times you might not understand." He added with a smile, "I even believe I am helping you in suggesting I should choose your gown for this evening. You should not be angry with me, you know."

She gave him a reluctant grin. "Maddening man! Do you usually get your own way?"

"I always get my own way," said the Marquis, laughing. "Never mind, my lady wife, you shall be the belle of the ball, that I promise."

The Marquis was as good as his word and Jennie was not only the belle of that ball but of many other balls and parties to follow. She was mildly puzzled by the absence of Guy from these occasions. She did so want him to see her in all her finery. Surely Guy moved in the same circles as the Marquis. Why, he had told her so himself, and Guy never lied.

But the novelty of wearing pretty dresses and being escorted everywhere by a handsome and complaisant husband and having Sally Byles in town as well, was enough to keep Jennie from thinking too much about the absent Guy.

She was delighted and relieved in a way to find that her husband had his own suite of rooms and showed no desire to share her bed. In fact, she told herself nightly how delighted she was and persuaded herself that her husband was no more than a bloodless man-milliner.

She confided as much to Sally Byles during an intimate coze and was amazed to see her friend's healthy country features stained with a painful blush.

"Perhaps I should not discuss such things with you Sally," said Jennie contritely. "But we have never had any secrets from each other."

"It's not that, Jennie," said Sally, looking worried. "Are you not frightened that your husband might look elsewhere for consolation?"

"Oh, Chemmy's not interested in women. He only cares for clothes," remarked Jennie rather smugly.

"You're *impossible*," Sally burst out. "Don't you know that Alice Waring was his mistress for years?"

Jennie stared at her. "Do you mean that very beautiful woman who attended my wedding?"

"Exactly."

"Oh," said Jennie in a small voice.

"It's all over, of course," said Sally quickly, feeling that her friend had suffered enough. "Mrs. Waring is now under the Earl of Freize's protection. But 'tis whispered that she is still in love with the Marquis."

Jennie was not old or wise enough to recognize jealousy when she felt it. She was only conscious of an overwhelming desire to prove to her husband that she was attractive to other men.

An opportunity placed itself in her way sooner than she expected.

She arose unusually early one morning and was descending the stairs to the morning room when, to her surprise, she heard the butler, Roberts, saying in a firm voice, "I am sorry Mr. Chalmers, my lord and lady are not at home."

"Guy!" cried Jennie, running down the stairs and darting past the startled butler. "Guy, my darling Guy. Of course I am at home."

She caught his hands and smiled radiantly up into his face. He looked thinner and older than she had remembered, but he was still her beloved Guy.

She ignored the stiff disapproval of the butler and drew Guy into the morning room, slamming the door behind them.

"I thought you had forgotten me," said Jennie.

"As if I could!" exclaimed Guy. "It's all the

fault of that cursed husband of yours. First, he takes you away to Kent forever and then he tells his servants to refuse me admittance."

"But I was never in Kent," said Jennie, puzzled. "He left me with my grandparents after the wedding."

"Well, if that don't beat all," said Guy wrathfully. "Look Jennie. Get your coat and bonnet. I'll take you for a drive. If we don't move quickly, your husband will be downstairs and we'll never have a chance to talk."

It took Jennie only a few minutes to collect her belongings, leave the house, and climb up into Guy's carriage.

He drove her to a secluded corner of Green Park and then reined in his horses.

An amazed Jennie heard his tale of journeying to Kent and how her husband had pretended she was with him.

"But I have been *everywhere* since I came to town," cried Jennie. "Why have I not seen you?" She began to reel off a list of notable names and houses and Guy scowled. He did not want to tell her that he was not in the habit of moving in such elevated circles.

"Oh, these things are a cursed bore," he said vaguely. "I tear up the invitations as soon as I get 'em. Let me look at you. God, but you're beautiful!"

He drew her into his arms and began to kiss her passionately. She finally pushed him away, feeling muddled and somehow guilty and forlorn. A large brown Jersey cow ambled over to the carriage and looked up at her accusingly.

"I am a married woman now, Guy," she said breathlessly. "We should not be doing this."

"What happened to your marriage of convenience?" sneered Guy. "I'll bet his lordship climbed into your bed as soon as possible."

"No!" cried Jennie, much flushed. "He has honored our arrangement. He has been most kind. And . . . and he has bought me all these pretty clothes."

"Well, that's one thing he should be good at," said Guy. "He certainly picked out a fine wardrobe for Alice Waring."

Jennie looked miserably down at her hands. She was being childish to hope that love should grow in such an odd marriage. She turned and sadly leaned her cheek against Guy's coat, hoping he would hold her and comfort her in the old brotherly way. But he caught her in his arms and began to kiss her in a way that made her feel excited and strange.

"We must see more of each other, Jennie," said Guy.

"It's difficult. My husband goes everywhere with me," replied Jennie, looking nervously around the park as if expecting to see the tall figure of her husband striding across the grass.

"You've a voice, haven't you," said Guy impatiently. "Use it! Tell him you do not need his escort everywhere. He will be happy to be free again to go to his club . . . or to the arms of Mrs. Waring."

Jennie gave a little sigh. Her reunion with Guy had not been as exciting and romantic as she had dreamed.

But he was all she had to cling to in a world which had gone unaccountably drab and gray. Why should her husband keep a mistress and yet expect her to behave herself? In her growing fury, she forgot all Sally's news that Mrs. Waring was now under someone else's protection.

"Look here," said Guy urgently. "I will meet you at the corner of Albemarle Street at the same time tomorrow. I know of a little place we can go to where we can be private . . . just to talk, you know," he added cleverly. "Just like old times."

"Very well," said Jennie. "We had better go back now, Guy, before anyone sees us."

The next morning Jennie crept quietly down the stairs and opened the hall door. It was all so easy! Her husband had not even mentioned Guy's visit.

It was a cold and glittering day with a high wind gusting great fleecy clouds across a pale blue sky.

Jennie paused on the doorstep to tuck her hands into her swansdown muff. The voice of her husband behind her nearly made her jump out of her boots.

"You should not go out unescorted," came Chemmy's languid voice from behind her. She turned slowly around. He was dressed to go out in a long frogged beaver coat. He had his curly brimmed hat perched at a jaunty angle on his fair hair and his cane tucked under his arm.

"I felt like g-going for a walk," stammered Jennie.

"Splendid!" said her husband. "We shall walk together. Nothing like walking, you know," he added conversationally, tucking her hand in his arm. "Clears the spleen and exercises the liver."

As they approached the corner of Albemarle Street, Jennie was all too conscious of the conspicuous figure of Guy, sitting perched on his carriage.

"Why, there is Mr. Chalmers," said the Marquis, politely bowing to that gentleman. "We must be setting the fashion for early rising, my dear. Good day, to you Chalmers. A splendid morning, is it not?"

Guy gave the couple a stiff bow, staring down at the top of Jennie's smart bonnet. She cast him one fleeting, anguished glance and then moved off around the corner on her husband's arm.

He sat there, holding the reins for what seemed an age, but was in fact only a few minutes, when he espied the Earl of Freize's two burly footmen ambling along the pavement towards him.

He slowly drew some gold from his pocket and began to toss it up and down in his hand so that the coins chinked merrily and flashed in the pale sunlight.

"I say you fellows," Guy cried, as they came abreast. "Perhaps you might like to perform a little commission for me."

"This is absolutely ridiculous," thought Jennie as they turned in at the gates of Green Park. Away from the shelter of the buildings, the wind appeared to be increasing in force by the minute and the blue sky was turning to gray. No clouds blew across but rather seemed to sink down through the blue to cover the heavens in a gray blanket.

The trees rattled their branches as they passed underneath and frost-edged leaves scurried and whispered over the grass.

Jennie covertly eyed her large husband from under the shade of her bonnet. A man so finely dressed and so concerned over the cut of his clothes could have very little stamina for anything so energetic as a brisk walk on a cold day. She had a sudden desire to show him what a useless and effete specimen of humanity he was.

"I love long walks," she said brightly, "but then I am a country girl. I never get tired so you must tell me when my energy begins to tax your . . . er . . . stamina." The latter was said with a faint tinge of contempt. Jennie glanced up at the blue eyes so far above her own and surprised that strange, slight narrowing of the pupils she thought she had imagined before at Runbury Manor. The next second, however, the eyes were bland and smiling.

"Thank you for your concern," he said, imperceptibly quickening his pace as they walked on together in silence.

Jennie's toes were beginning to freeze in the thin leather of her boots and her nose was turning an unbecoming pink.

Her lord strolled along beside her as if he were taking a walk on the finest of summer days. He was still holding her arm in a firm clasp and his nearness made her feel uncomfortable. She had hardly ever been completely alone with her husband. At home, there were always the servants, and at balls and parties there were several hundred people packed around them, elbow to elbow.

She thought of the beautiful Alice Waring. She was sure Mrs. Waring's nose never turned red with cold. She felt like a drab and longed for Guy, with his reassuring compliments and kisses.

"This is a splendid idea of yours, Jennie," said the Marquis after they had been walking for about an hour. "I feel like a new man. We must do this every morning. Is anything the matter, my heart? I could swear you groaned. No? In that case let us walk some more. I declare, it is beginning to snow. I love snow. It brings out the schoolboy in me. So pretty. But the squirrels will go back to their trees. See that little fellow, Jennie. See how daintily he holds that nut in his little paws."

Jennie privately enjoyed some unladylike thoughts about the squirrel and contented herself with murmuring "Yes" through frozen lips.

They had almost reached the gates when, to Jennie's horror, her husband blithely swung around and began to march her back into the park at a brisk trot. Feathery snow flakes gathered on her eyelashes. He was taking her down a deserted path under some old trees which moaned and rattled in the wind. Jennie was about to give up and plead that she could not endure the cold one more minute, when she saw to her dismay that two burly men had crept out from behind the trees and were blocking their path.

The footmen had held off their attack for the last hour. They had recognized their quarry as the Marquis of Charrington and were fearful of being recognized themselves. But the thickening snow had given them courage. A few blows with their cudgels and the Marquis would be down. And then they could collect the other half of their money from Guy.

Jennie let out a squeak of terror. The Marquis pushed her behind him, never taking his eyes from the two men.

It was then that Jennie did what she always afterwards considered a most shameful thing. She picked up her skirts and ran. Ran through the now heavily falling snow, gasping and panting with fright, until she reached the edge of the park. There was no sound of pursuit.

She hung on to a tree trunk for dear life until she had recovered her breath.

It was then she realized what she had done. She had abandoned her husband to the mercy of two thugs who would no doubt kill him. She, who had always prided herself on her courage, had run away and left Chemmy to die.

She whirled around and began to run back the way she had come. "Let him only be alive," she prayed, "and I will never see Guy again."

But trees and snow seemed to dance in front of her eyes in a bewildering pattern. She could not find the path where her husband had been attacked.

A huge figure suddenly loomed up out of the snow in front of her and she threw back her head and screamed.

"It's me, dear heart," said a familiar voice and familiar arms were wrapped around her.

"There, do not cry," said the Marquis. "Did you think I would abandon you? I came in search of you immediately."

This was too much for the guilty Jennie, who began to sob, "How can I ever forgive myself. I ran away and left you. I thought you would be killed."

"Of course not," he teased. "Would you like me to show you the bodies?"

"Oh, are they *dead?*"

"No, just stunned."

"How did you . . . how could you . . ."

"Never mind," he said, leading her towards the park gates. "Let us go home."

"Oh, let's," sobbed Jennie. "I am so cold and miserable. I-I foolishly hoped to punish you. I thought you would feel the cold before I did. I am so tired, too."

"Now, why do you want to punish me?" he asked.

"I d-don't know," said Jennie, beginning to cry in earnest.

"You are overwrought," he said kindly. "And you do not know what you are saying."

How splendid it was to return home to blazing fires and hot drinks and hot food! Jennie had bathed and changed and was sitting with her feet up on the fender in the sitting room when her husband entered carrying a book.

"I never see you reading," he began. "You must feel free to use my library any time you wish. Here is a copy of Mrs. Radcliffe's *Count Ugolino*. I know it is the fashion to despise novels, but many ladies appear to enjoy this one. Have you read it?"

Jennie shook her head.

"Do but glance at the first page and see if you think it would amuse you."

He then looked at his wife curiously. She was staring at the volume as if it were a species of poisonous snake. She reluctantly turned to the opening chapter and stared fixedly at the page, her face growing redder and redder.

He studied her thoughtfully. Her eyes were staring straight at the print, moving neither to right nor left.

"As you can see," he said in a gentle voice, "the heroine is called Sally, just like your friend."

"Yes, indeed," cried Jennie, staring at the page.

He moved forwards and took the book from

her trembling fingers. "There is no Sally, my dear. You cannot read." The latter remark was a statement rather than a question.

Jennie bowed her head and the hot tears of shame began to roll down her cheeks. It had not taken her long since her arrival in London to realize that her unlettered state was the exception rather than the rule.

He put a long finger under her chin and drawing out his handkerchief gently dried her eyes. "The shame is your grandparents, not yours. It can be easily remedied. I shall hire you a tutor this very day."

"I don't want a tutor," said Jennie pettishly. "Guy says there is no reason for a lady to read or write."

Her husband picked up Mrs. Radcliffe's book. "As you will," he said amiably and left the room, quietly closing the doors behind him.

Jennie stared at the doors and bit her lip. What was *wrong* with her? For some silly whim — for some stupid reason she was unable to fathom, she had condemned herself to a life of illiteracy.

She slowly got to her feet and went in search of her husband. He was seated at a desk in his study and he did not turn his head when she entered the room.

Jennie stared at his elegant back and tried to summon up her courage. Then she noticed that his hand, grasping the quill pen, was bruised and the skin was broken over the knuckles.

"What happened to your hand?" she cried,

feeling a strange stab of concern.

"You cannot expect me to fight two gentlemen in Green Park and come off unscathed," he said.

Jennie flushed guiltily. She had not believed he had routed his two assailants. She had thought the thugs had somehow changed their minds and fled.

She looked at her husband with dawning respect. He got to his feet and looked down at her with a certain lazy amusement in his blue eyes.

"Did you want to see me about something, dear heart?"

"I would like a tutor, after all," said Jennie, her eyes dropping before his gaze.

"Then you shall have one," he said, kissing her gently on the corner of her mouth.

He always manages to make me feel guilty, thought Jennie. *Why does he never reproach me? His feelings for me are not strong enough,* she decided, feeling all of a sudden very flat.

"I shall not be free this evening to escort you to the Hambledon ball. Shall I ask Perry to stand in for me?"

"You should not be so concerned," said Jennie. " 'Tis not fashionable to be seen everywhere with one's husband. Guy shall take me. I suppose you want to go to your club."

"Perhaps," he said. "But you cannot have Mr. Chalmers to escort you. He is not invited."

"Nonsense!" said Jennie. "Guy is invited everywhere. He simply finds all these occasions too dull."

"Perry shall escort you — or no one," said her husband equably.

Jennie stamped her foot. "Then I won't go at all!" she cried. "I shall stay at home and sew."

"As you will," said her husband in his usual infuriating manner. He sat down at his desk and began to write.

Jennie stared for a few fulminating seconds at his well-tailored back and then noisily exited from the study, slamming the door behind her.

She spent a long and boring afternoon in her sitting room. If only she had a dictionary. Then she could send a note to Guy. But even if she could find one in the library, it would take her ages to complete even one sentence.

The street door slammed and Jennie crossed to the window. She had an excellent view of her husband as he climbed up into his carriage and took the reins. The snow had ceased to fall and was already beginning to melt into dingy slush.

The Marquis called to his butler who was standing on the pavement by the carriage, "I shall not be back until very late tonight. There is no need to wait up for me."

Jennie turned from the window as a diminutive housemaid came in and began to make up the fire.

Jennie eyed the little girl with sudden hope.

"What is your name?" she asked.

"Perkins, my lady."

"Well, Perkins, I have a letter to write but I am suffering from severe eye strain," lied Jennie.

"Do you know anyone in the household who could pen a note for me?"

"*I* could, my lady," said Perkins brightly. "I was taught at parochial school."

Oh, the injustices of society, thought Jennie. Here she was, a peeress of His Majesty's realm, having to ask a housemaid to write a letter.

Soon a carefully distant and formal message begging Mr. Chalmers to call was sent around to his lodgings.

Jennie eagerly hung about the hall, frightened that the stern butler would tell Guy she was not at home.

At last he arrived. His first words startled Jennie. "I gather the Marquis is indisposed," he said cheerfully, allowing the disapproving butler to relieve him of his drab benjamin.

"He is in the best of health," said Jennie. "What made you think he would be ill? You look ill yourself, Guy. You've gone quite white. He *could* have been killed, however. Two terrible thugs set upon him in the park. But he knocked them senseless," added Jennie with a trace of pride in her voice.

"Forget about that," said Guy hurriedly. He suddenly seemed anxious to be off. "What did you want to see me about?"

Jennie simply looked confused. She had wanted comfort and reassurance. She had wanted to punish her husband. But Guy upset her, standing as he did, shuffling from foot to foot and shying like a frightened horse every

91

time a carriage passed on the street outside.

"I just wanted to see you," said Jennie plaintively. "Being married feels so strange and we never have much time together as we did in the old days, Guy." She put her hand on his sleeve and stared up, almost timidly, into his face as if willing him to become the old Guy — half brother, half lover.

A man's voice sounded from the street outside and a horse neighed and stamped.

"Tell you what, Jennie," said Guy quickly. "I know of a place where we can spend the evening together. Here . . . I'll write a note . . . oh, blast, I haven't got time to do it. Just remember it. It's a place called the White Swan, a posting house just beyond Highgate on the Barnet Road. Come there tomorrow night. I shall send a carriage for you. We shall have a cozy supper together and talk about old times."

"But Chemmy . . ." wailed Jennie.

"Did you get rid of him this evening?" countered Guy. "Yes. I thought so. Well, do it again tomorrow night."

Still Jennie hesitated. Guy's manner seemed excited and strange.

"Don't worry about that husband of yours," said Guy, shrewdly noticing her hesitation. "He's probably in the arms of Alice Waring right now."

Jennie remembered Sally's words. "But Guy," she protested, "that affair is now over. Mrs. Waring is in the protection of the Earl of Freize."

"And who says she can't have two lovers?" sneered Guy.

Jennie's face went pale and pinched. What a messy sordid world it had turned out to be. Why couldn't people just get married and remain loyal to each other?

There was a sharp rap on the knocker of the street door and Jennie gulped and jumped guiltily.

"Hurry, Jennie," said Guy urgently. "Give me your answer."

"Mr. Deighton," announced the butler from the doorway.

Perry's slightly protruding eyes flicked across Guy for one brief second and settled on Jennie. "My lady," he said, bowing low. "I came in the hope of finding your husband at home."

"I-I think you will find him at one of his clubs," said Jennie, throwing Guy an anguished look.

"Good evening, Deighton," said Guy in a hearty voice, but the dapper little man kept his eyes fixed on Jennie.

"Thank you, my lady," he replied. "I shall go in search of him."

Jennie blushed miserably. The air seemed to be thick with censure. "Can I offer you some refreshment, Mr. Deighton?" she asked.

"That is very kind of you," said Perry primly. "I am pleased to accept." He sat down neatly on a sofa. "I thought you would have been at the Hambledon ball. I called there and was surprised to find you absent."

"Oh, Jennie didn't care to go," said Guy. "The Hambledons can be monstrous dull."

Perry looked at him for the first time. "I am surprised you know the Hambledons well enough to form any opinion of them at all, Mr. Chalmers," he said coldly.

Jennie flew to Guy's defense. "Guy is invited everywhere," she cried.

"No, he isn't," said Perry forthrightly, "especially after that . . ."

"I must go, Jennie," interrupted Guy hurriedly. "What is your answer?"

"Yes," said Jennie, staring coldly at Mr. Deighton, who was sitting very still and upright on the backless sofa, emanating waves of distaste and dislike.

"Very well," said Guy, kissing her cheek.

Perry watched him leave. He looked about to burst.

"How *can* you," he exclaimed when the door had closed behind Guy. "How *can* you entertain *such* a man?"

"Mr. Chalmers is my cousin," said Jennie in freezing accents.

"That's no reason to know him," pointed out Perry. "Every family's got a loose screw in it somewhere."

Jennie completely lost her temper. "You horrid little, *little* man," she spluttered. "Take yourself off." She suddenly recoiled as Perry jumped to his feet. No one had ever before dared to call the fire-eater that was Mr. Deighton "little." He was abnormally sensitive about his lack of inches.

"I would rather be *little* and remain loyal to my sex," he said acidly. "You, my virgin bride, are not even a woman. Pah! No wonder poor Chemmy has to seek his pleasures elsewhere. You have neither grace nor wit nor loyalty nor femininity. You have the mind of a trollop atop a frigid body, madame. Chemmy has my sincere pity."

"How dare you!" screamed Jennie, jumping up and down with rage. *"Get out.* Out, out, out, *out!"* She picked up a pretty figurine and flung it full at him.

Perry caught it neatly, put it down gently on a side table and walked to the doors. He swung around.

"Your incestuous relationship with your cousin disgusts me, madame. You do not belong in society. You belong to the demimonde. Good day to you!"

He closed the doors with a hearty bang and Jennie dissolved into tears. No one had ever said such harsh and horrible things to her before. It was all Chemmy's fault. Everyone had liaisons, didn't they?

But for the first time she heard the disturbing voice of her conscience and began to feel afraid.

Chapter Six

"The provocation was great, look you!" said Mr. Peregrine Deighton.

The Marquis of Charrington eyed him with mild surprise. He had returned home in the small hours of the morning to be told by a sleepy butler that Mr. Deighton had been waiting for him in the drawing room since midnight.

"Whose been provoking you, Perry?" said the Marquis lazily. "Do you want me to act as your second?"

"I was provoked by a lady," said Perry.

The Marquis had been in the act of helping himself to a glass of canary from the decanter. He put the glass down on the silver tray with a little click and said in a deceptively mild voice, "And what did my dear wife say to you?"

"She . . . she called me 'little,' " said Perry.

"To which you replied . . . ?"

"To which I replied that she had the mind of a trollop atop a frigid body," said Perry miserably.

The Marquis stood very still. "Harsh words, dear friend," he said at last in the soft, gentle voice that Perry knew meant he was very angry indeed. "You will sit just where you are, Perry, and begin at the beginning and go on to the end."

Perry hung his head and then began to repeat

96

all that had been said, word for word.

"My wife is young and heedless," said the Marquis when he had finished, "but mark this, my friend. This is as much her house as mine and whom she chooses to entertain here is of concern only to Jennie and myself. You will write my wife a letter of apology, Perry. The provocation, as you say, was great. But she is a young, untried girl and you are a mature gentleman of the world. I value your friendship and loyalty but it does not give you license to insult my wife. Do I make myself plain?"

"Yes," mumbled Perry.

"But one thing intrigues me. Chalmers asked her for her answer and she said 'yes.' Are you sure that was all?"

Perry nodded miserably.

The Marquis poured out two glasses of the pale yellow liquid and handed one to his friend. "Very well," he said. "Come! Do not look so gloomy, my friend. You have confessed all like an officer and gentleman. We shall consider the matter closed. I attended the Hambledons' ball after all. I did not arrive till midnight but it was still a sad crush. Brummell was there with Alvanley. He said a vastly amusing thing. . . ."

The Marquis chatted on in his lazy voice of this and that until he saw the embarrassment and unease leaving his friend's face.

But the Marquis was only human after all. As Perry began to chat in his turn, the Marquis stretched his long legs to the fire and wondered happily how his wife had enjoyed being called frigid.

Jennie had lain awake until about half an hour before the Marquis arrived home, burning for revenge. The Marquis should challenge his friend to a duel at the very least. She then fell into a heavy sleep where she dreamed she was back at the Manor being visited by the Marquis, who had Alice Waring on his arm and who was denying in his usual lazy and indifferent way that he had ever been married.

Jennie woke to the sunlight of a clear, early winter's day. She hurriedly dressed and ran lightly down the stairs to look for her husband, only to be informed that he was still abed.

She paced restlessly through the rooms, waiting for him to appear and finally went in search of him.

She pushed open the door of his bedroom and stood for a moment on the threshold. He was lying in a lofty four-poster bed, quietly and completely asleep. Jennie moved slowly forward, held on to one of the elaborately turned and carved posts and stared down at her lord's placid face. She gave a loud cough but still he slept on. She moved up to the head of the bed and leaned over, looking closely at his face, as if hoping he might betray some of his real feelings in sleep.

His eyes suddenly opened wide, looking strangely intelligent and alert, but the next

second were registering all his usual amiable indifference.

"Good morning, dear heart," he said sitting up
in bed and affording Jennie an excellent view of
his naked chest. "I see by your beautiful sparkling eyes that you cannot wait to tell me of
Perry's insults and misdeeds. But before you
speak, do bring me that letter . . . over on my
dresser."

Jennie opened her mouth to snap that she had
no intention of listening to him read any letter but
she was nonplussed by the sight of her half-naked
husband and his imperturbable good humor.
"Go on," he urged gently, removing his nightcap
and running his long fingers through his hair.

She flushed in embarrassment, walked over to
the dresser and picked up the letter. Her husband read it out loud. Perry had indeed written
an abject apology. It would be churlish and unladylike not to accept it. Jennie found herself
furious that the wind had been taken so neatly
out of her sails. "You always have an answer to
everything," she remarked bitterly. "Well, answer
me this. How long do you intend to flaunt your
relationship with Mrs. Waring in front of me?"

"I stopped . . . er . . . flaunting Mrs. Waring before we were married, my heart," said the Marquis with lazy amusement. "I would not for a
minute consider flaunting anyone in front of you
. . . even one of my female relatives."

"I didn't think you had any," said Jennie, mo-
mentarily diverted.

"I have a few maiden aunts and distant cousins. Apart from that, I am all alone in the world. What are your plans for the day?"

Jennie looked at him cautiously. "I-I thought I would spend the evening with Sally," she said. "Just me. I mean . . . girls' gossip, you know, you would be frightfully bored."

"You never bore me," he said simply. "Come and kiss me, Jennie."

"No!" she squeaked, backing toward the door.

"Dear me," said his lordship with unimpaired good humor, leaning back against the pillows of the high bed. "I believe you are frightened of me."

"Nonsense!" said Jennie roundly. "It is just that I am not in the way of being intimate with you."

"I was not asking for any great degree of intimacy," he said mildly. "I simply asked for a kiss."

"Oh, well, if that is all," said Jennie ungraciously. She moved towards the bed and dabbed a kiss on his cheek, but he took her by the shoulders and held her gently away from him, looking at her flushed face and downcast eyes.

Then he bent his head very slowly and kissed her gently on the mouth. Jennie backed away from him, feeling dizzy and upset. It had been a kiss, no more, but it had left her feeling strangely trembly and weak. She would have turned and fled but his next words stopped her.

"Your tutor will be here in an hour," he said. "He is a Scotchman of some learning, I believe.

His name is Mr. Porteous."

The Marquis swung his long muscular legs out of bed and Jennie gave a choked sound of shock. She ran out of the room as fast as she could.

When he descended the stairs an hour later, he paused outside the drawing room from which came the sound of Mr. Porteous' voice, "Now, now, my leddy," he was admonishing his new pupil, "just a wee bit mair patience and you will have penned your furst sentence."

The Marquis grinned and then turned as he saw his butler, Roberts, crossing the hall with a small note folded into a triangle which he had placed on a silver salver. "For my lady," said Roberts.

"I will take it to her," said the Marquis, picking up the billet but, instead of entering the drawing room, he went back upstairs.

He closed the door of his private sitting room behind him and stood looking down at the letter in his hand. It was sealed with a lurid purple wax and the seal itself showed a rather groggy griffin rampant. He crossed the room to his dressing case and took out a razor. Then he lit a candle and held the long Sheffield steel blade over the flame. He neatly slid the hot blade through the wax and carefully opened the letter so as not to break any more of the seal.

The letter read, "Dear Coz, I shall be waiting for you at the White Swan which is in the village of Harham, beyond Highgate on the Barnet Road. The coach will call for you at five. Do not fail me. Your humble and adoring . . . Guy."

The Marquis studied his reflection in the mirror. "I wonder," he murmured, "I *really* wonder how I would look with a pair of horns. But I have no mind to play the cuckold."

He frowned suddenly and stared down at the letter in his hands.

Although Chemmy was apt to maneuver towards a desired goal with the single-minded tenacity of the English aristocracy, he had escaped much of that breed's insensitivity. His instinct was to trust Jennie. His instinct also told him that Jennie would never be unfaithful to him, no matter how many Guys came upon the scene. It would be better to let Jennie find out for herself just how weak and devious her cousin was. "The more I leave her alone," he thought, "the more likely she is to come about. But on the other hand, he could not leave her at Guy's mercy. It is time to take some action!"

He carefully folded the letter back into its triangular shape and gently heated the wax, this time with the blunt edge of the razor, and deftly molded the seal back into shape.

He then ran lightly down the stairs and entered the drawing room.

Jennie was sitting at a pretty Hepplewhite secretaire. There was an ink blot on her cheek and her face was flushed with concentration. Mr. Porteous, a grizzled middle-aged man with craggy features and small twinkling eyes was watching her indulgently. Chemmy crossed to his wife's side and silently handed her the note, which she slid under her book like a guilty child.

He was greatly tempted to stay and insist she open it, but he fought against it and kissed her lightly on the cheek instead.

Jennie watched him leave. She felt terrible. If only she had not promised to meet Guy.

"Well, back to your lessons, my leddy," said the voice of her tutor, Mr. Porteous. "I have here an interesting observation by Montaigne, I would like you to write. Now, just copy my handwriting as best you can and then we'll finish for the day. Oh, I'll read you what it says first so you'll know what it is you're writing about. Let me see . . . mphm . . . Montaigne says here in his Essays, 'Marriage may be compared to a cage: the birds outside despair to get in and those within despair to get out.' Aye, just so. Shall we begin?"

Guy Chalmers stood at the edge of Harham village duck pond and watched the winter sun drowning in its glassy waters.

He lit a cheroot and felt at ease with the winter world which stretched around him in the evening light like a symphony in monochrome. The pale gold of thatch on the low houses huddled on the edge of the village green shone in the dying rays of the sun. Tall brown reeds stood sentinel at the water's edge and great trees etched their brown patterns against a gray and yellow sky. Beside the water one scarlet leaf, brave survivor of autumn, blazed like a jewel among all the golds and browns. Behind him stood the inn, emanating warm smells of beer and roast beef. He fingered the bottle of laudanum in his pocket. He would slip a large measure of it into Jennie's wine and then escort her to that bedroom he had so thoughtfully bespoken.

He blew a smoke ring in the air and was contemplating feeding the glowing end of his cheroot to a passing duck when a mighty kick in the rear-end sent him flying into the shallow pond.

He floundered and gasped and struggled to get up. A massive blow from a mighty fist struck him behind the ear and he fell senseless into the water. A pair of strong hands dragged him into the shelter of the reeds and turned his white and senseless face up to the evening sky.

The shadow of the coach he had hired for Jennie swept over his body and the long thin shadows of the reeds cast bars across his face.

In the cozy inn parlor, Jennie, Marchioness of Charrington, warmed her hands with a glass of negus and wondered what on earth had happened to Guy. Through the leaded windows of the inn she could see candles beginning to flicker in the windows of the village cottages. She was painfully aware of the fact she was unescorted and was glad that the parlor was as yet devoid of other customers, although cheerful masculine voices were beginning to resound from the taproom beyond.

She wondered if Perkins, the housemaid, had read Guy's letter for her aright. Perhaps she had mistaken the time.

The little cloud of guilt which had been hanging around Jennie's head all day gathered into a full-sized storm and seemed to burst upon her. She should *never* have come. She resolutely gathered up her reticule and gloves and, leaving a little silver on the table to pay for her negus, prepared to return to London.

But there was no sign of her coach. A cheeky ostler told her that the coachman had taken off at a great rate saying "as he didn't hold with wiolence, not him." And while Jennie stared at him in horror, wondering what on earth he could mean, a familiar voice sounded in her ears. "What a surprise! Jennie, my love!"

Jennie spun around and found the great bulk of her husband towering over her.

"W-what are y-you doing here?" she babbled.

"I have been visiting some friends in Barnet," he replied in his usual amiable, pleasant drawl. His face was in the shadow.

"I-I w-was doing the same thing exactly," lied Jennie desperately. "I decided to go and visit my old nurse who is . . . or was . . . retired here. Alas, the poor dear died some time ago and my stupid Jehu . . . I hired a carriage, you see . . . he ups and goes back to London, leaving me stranded."

"Amazing!" said his lordship, without so much as a trace of mockery in his voice. "We can travel back to town together and, since you have obviously decided to forgo your call to Sally, perhaps you would care to spend a quiet evening at home with me?"

"Oh, yes," said Jennie faintly. "And do let us leave *now*."

She was suddenly afraid that Guy might arrive and prove her story a lie.

The Marquis threw a coin to the ostler and they waited in silence until the carriage was brought around, led by the wooden-faced groom, John.

Jennie, who knew that a lady *never* expects a gentleman to help her up onto the box of his carriage when he is driving it himself, waited until the Marquis was seated with the reins in his hands and then nipped up nimbly beside him.

She wrapped herself in the rugs thoughtfully provided for her by the groom.

She became aware that the carriage showed no signs of moving. The Marquis was staring in the direction of the pond. Suddenly he gave a little sigh of satisfaction, bent and kissed his wife hard on the mouth in such a way as to leave her feeling breathless and strangely exhilarated.

Chemmy sprang his horses and the carriage swept in a half circle past the village pond and off in the direction of London.

The muddy, weed-covered, shivering and abject figure that was Guy Chalmers heaved himself up from the mud pond and stared after them with a rage in his heart as black as the sky above.

Jennie looked down the long length of the dining table and covertly surveyed her husband. Although they were dining at home, he had changed into a faultless evening coat and knee breeches. He had been chatting lazily of this and that. Jennie, now that she had got over her shock, felt those old familiar stirrings of contempt. What proper *man* would have accepted such a cock and bull story as the one that she had told about her nurse? Jennie had never even considered for a moment that her husband might have somehow read her note from Guy. The Marquis caught her eye and lovingly smoothed the sleeve of his coat.

"Do you like this, my heart?" he asked anxiously. "I had it made for me by Weston and he claims it is his masterpiece."

"Very fine," said his wife, with a slight curl to her lip.

"I am so glad you like it," he said in the earnest voice that he only used when talking about clothes. "Did I tell you we shall be traveling into the country tomorrow? No! Dear me. How remiss of me. Yes, I feel it is high time we paid a call on your . . . er . . . *beloved* home."

It was Jennie's day for feeling guilty. She had not really thought much about her grandparents since she had come to town. The thought of her former dirty home with its comfortless rooms and terrible meals made her want to shudder.

"I wish you would not make such arrangements without consulting me first," she snapped.

Chemmy raised his thin eyebrows in surprise. "Had I thought for a *minute* that the idea would be repugnant to you, of *course*, I would naturally have consulted you. But since your love for your home was strong enough to make you want to spend your wedding night there, I naturally assumed . . ."

"Then you shouldn't," said Jennie pettishly, throwing down her napkin.

"Poor Jennie," he said, getting lazily to his feet and strolling around the table towards her. "You shall just have to make the best of it. Your grandparents are expecting you."

"I do not like having a master," said Jennie mulishly.

"Do you mean *me?*" cried Chemmy, taking her in his arms and clutching her to his bosom in what she uneasily felt was a deliberately theatrical manner. "I worship the ground you walk on. I kiss your feet . . . or rather I would if my jacket would but allow me to bend."

"Oh, *you* . . . you *fop*," said Jennie, struggling to release herself and hoping against hope that she had gone too far this time and that her seemingly emotionless husband would at least be provoked into a show of anger, but his blue eyes merely glinted with amusement as he gazed down into her flushed face.

"How true and, oh, how sad," he said, holding her very close, so close that she could feel the hard muscles of his legs pressing against her own. He began to kiss her very lightly and expertly, her eyes, her nose, her mouth, her breast and her mouth again until she gave a choked moaning sound in the back of her throat and clutched desperately at the silk revers of his evening coat for support.

"Oh, Jennie," he sighed huskily, "there is something I must tell you, my heart."

"What is it, Chemmy?" she breathed, staring up into his handsome face with a drowned look in her eyes.

"You are clutching me so hard, you are quite spoiling the set of my coat," said the Marquis.

"Damn your bloody coat, sirrah, and damn and double damn *you*," howled his little wife, wrenching herself out of his arms and fleeing from the room.

The Marquis looked after her disappearing figure and a smile curled his mobile mouth. "Yes, I really must buy you a horse, my lady wife," he murmured, "for you have obviously had a close acquaintanceship with the stables!"

Chapter Seven

For a long time afterward, Jennie was to associate bright sunshine with disaster. Not for her the Gothic omens of the thunderstorm, with its jagged flashes of lightning and purple clouds.

When she and her husband drove up to the ivy-covered front of Runbury Manor, brilliant sunshine was flooding the ragged estate and the birds were chirping busily in the trees, ruffling their feathers under the benison of a mock spring day.

The groom, John, performed a cheerful rat-tat-tat on the door knocker and Jennie and the Marquis stood side by side on the mossy steps, waiting for someone to answer.

Silence.

No omens. No warnings. Only the busy chattering of the birds in the ivy and the dry rattle of crumpled dead leaves over the frozen gravel of the drive.

John banged on the knocker again and then tried the door which swung open revealing the darkness of the hall beyond.

The smell of the cold, fetid air was like a blow in the face.

On an old, high-backed carved chair in the hall sat the elderly footman, dressed in his finery of the last century. His thin, spindly legs in their clocked stockings were neatly crossed, his frail, gloved hands rested motionless in his lap and his pale old eyes stared blankly into space.

Jennie would have run to him but the Marquis held her back. "He is dead," said Chemmy quietly. "I do not know what has been going on here, my dear, but the stench is appalling. You must wait outside in the carriage for me."

Too shocked to argue, Jennie stumbled out of the door and took in great gulps of the clear, cold winter air outside.

She climbed into the traveling carriage and wrapped herself in rugs, willing herself not to think. Not to think at all.

After what seemed like an age, the Marquis walked slowly from the house, followed by John and climbed in beside her.

He took her small gloved hands in his own. "Your grandparents are dead," he said in an emotionless voice. "I found Martha, the cook, and some of the remaining servants in the kitchens in a bad state of shock.

"They say they had pleaded with Lord Charles to hire men to clear the cesspool but he stubbornly insisted it was a waste of money. The other night when it was very cold, he had a sudden fit of extravagance and ordered the servants to close all the windows and light fires in every room and keep them burning all night. Your grandparents and several of the servants died of asphyxiation."

Jennie clung to his hands, unable to take in the shattering news. People died of such causes every day of the year but it was hard to understand that it could happen to anyone one knew.

"And Jeffries . . . the footman?" whispered Jennie.

"I think he died of a broken heart," said Chemmy gently. "He was the one who discovered your grandparents dead. He then dressed himself in his best livery and sat himself in that chair in the hall . . . as if on duty . . . and waited for death to arrive."

"I must go to them," said Jennie.

"There is nothing you can do," said her husband, pressing her back into the seat. "John will convey you to the nearest inn while I attend to all that is necessary here. Believe me, my heart, you will only distress yourself beyond reason. You must leave things to me."

Jennie nodded dumbly. "The dogs are dead too, poor brutes," said the Marquis, "and unless I remove the rest of the old servants quickly, I will not answer for their lives. Please go, Jennie. John will take care of you until I arrive."

Jennie sat as rigidly as a statue as the carriage jolted down the rutted drive. She was tortured with guilt.

"I hardly ever thought of them these past weeks," she murmured aloud. "Perhaps I could have saved them had I been more dutiful. Oh, poor Guy, he will suffer as much as I, for he loved them dearly."

The image of the Guy of her childhood came back before her eyes, gentle and smiling, and she suddenly ached for his comforting presence.

As soon as she reached her rooms at the local inn, Jennie sat down to write a letter to Guy. She and no one else must break the terrible news to him. After all, he was all she had to cling to now, the only family she had left.

Guy Chalmers put down the tear-stained letter with a triumphant smile and slowly swung around to face his visitor, Alice Waring.

Alice had decided to call on Guy before attending Almack's subscription ball. She no longer bore Guy any ill-will, having felt that the Earl of Freize had settled the score for her by humiliating Guy that night at the opera. Despite the chill of the evening, she was wearing a pale pink Indian muslin gown, damped to reveal the most of her charms. Diamonds — a gift from the Earl — blazed at her throat and in her hair.

She had called on Guy since she still nourished a curiosity about the Marquis' marriage and the arrival of Jennie's letter had interrupted her questions.

"You look like the cat that swallowed the canary," she laughed. "Has someone left you a fortune?"

"By God, I think they have," said Guy exultantly. "My dear cousin informs me that those old quizzes, Lord and Lady Bemyss, have gone to meet their Maker. Lord Charles didn't hold with females inheriting money and he had the good sense to pop off before Jennie produced any brats. Oh, my stars! How rich he must have been! Stupid old miser."

"Often people considered by all the world to have been misers shock them by dying and revealing that they were, in fact, abysmally poor all along," said Alice scornfully.

"Not he," cried Guy. "Look you, I used to wait until he had his afternoon nap and I would check his business papers. Anyway, mean as he was, he never raised the tenants' taxes or rents in all his long lifetime. By George! What a shock they will receive when *I* arrive on the scene. I'll have every man Jack of them paying double."

"Yes," murmured Alice. "I can see you in the role of wicked landlord, throwing widows and orphans out into the snow."

"So," went on Guy with a sneer, "you can take yourself off, my dear doxy. I have no more use for you!"

"You never were any use anyway," said Alice, her good humor unimpaired. "You are not much of a man."

"Get out!" said Guy with a dangerous glint in his eye.

"Oh, I'm going, I'm going," said Alice. "But, hark on, Guy Chalmers. Insult me no further or I shall tell that cousin of yours of your true nature."

"What do I care?" laughed Guy. "Tell the world and his wife! Rich people like me do not need to worry about social blandishments."

Alice shivered and pulled her ermine cloak up around her bare shoulders. "Well, my late collaborator," she said, rising languidly to her feet, "think on this piece of advice, for I have learned it in a hard school. Wish revenge and hate on the world and that is exactly what you will get back . . . doublefold. Good day to you, *Mr. Chalmers.*"

But Guy's head was once more bent over the letter and a smile of triumph played on his lips.

Just wait until that will was read!

The will was read three days after the funeral of Lord and Lady Bemyss, in the drawing room of the Marquis of Charrington's town house.

Only Jennie, Guy and the Marquis were present. The lawyer, Mr. Humphreys, was even older than his late client and his thin, frail voice echoed around the room as he at last began to read from the papers in front of him. Snow fell gently outside the windows.

Mr. Humphreys began with a long list of bequests to Lord Charles' old servants, many of whom, Guy was pleased to note, were already dead.

He suddenly heard the sound of his name and sat very still. "To Mr. Guy Chalmers I leave five hundred guineas with the earnest plea that he will not immediately dissipate it in some low gambling hell." And as Guy sat rigid with shock, the elderly voice went on. "The bulk of my estate, I leave to my dear granddaughter, Jennifer, Marchioness of Charrington, secure in the knowledge that it will be expertly managed for her by her husband. . . ." The voice droned on, describing the extent of Lord Charles' fortune in detail. Guy had been right in only one thing. Lord Charles had, indeed, been a very wealthy man.

Guy felt he would die of an apoplexy. The will had said "Jennifer, Marchioness of Charrington" and had therefore been changed after Jennie's marriage. But he would never achieve the revenge he thirsted for if he showed his hate. As Shakespeare so rightly said, "One may smile and smile, and be a villain." He was about to turn around in his chair to twinkle boyishly at Jennie who, he knew, was seated behind him by the fireplace, when the voice of the lawyer again caught his attention.

"Should my beloved granddaughter, Jennifer, die childless, then the bulk of my estate, my moneys and my properties will pass to my great-nephew, Mr. Guy Chalmers."

Chemmy stood by the fireplace, leaning his arm along the mantle and watching the back of Guy's head. He suddenly wished very much to see his face.

When the reading of the will was over, Jennie was inclined to be tearful and apologetic to Guy. How wicked of Grandpapa! He should have left dear Guy more. And Guy smiled and disclaimed.

As the Marquis led Mr. Humphreys out to the hall, Guy waited until he was out of earshot and then playfully seized Jennie by the hands and swung her around.

"Poor Jennie," he said ruefully. "Had Lord Charles only died a little earlier, you would not have had to endure this farce of a marriage!"

"Oh, Grandpapa!" said Jennie, her eyes filling with tears. "No, I do not complain about my marriage, Guy. I am *glad* I married Chemmy now. At least before he died, Grandpapa had no worries about me."

Little hypocrite, thought Guy viciously. But he said aloud in a tender voice, "Ah, how brave you are, my little cousin. I shall always be here by your side, Jennie, to take care of you. You know I love you and will always care for you." He dropped her hands abruptly as Chemmy strolled into the room.

"I must speed you on your way, Chalmers," said the Marquis amiably. "My wife has been under a considerable strain these past few days and I feel she should rest."

"Of course," said Guy, all solicitation. He pressed Jennie's hand to his lips, bowed to the Marquis and took his leave suddenly anxious to be alone — to plot and plan.

Although Guy called assiduously at the mansion in Albemarle Street, he was steadfastly refused admittance. Her ladyship was always "resting." Jennie had, in fact, settled into a solitary life, mourning for her dead grandparents, having found out too late how much she had loved them. Her husband was an easy and undemanding companion and her tutor, Mr. Porteous, called daily to further her education.

A blustery spring blew past and soon the London Season came around again. Jennie began to dress in half-mourning and the Marquis informed her that it would be quite in order for her to attend balls and parties, provided she did not dance.

All of a sudden, Jennie was anxious to be out in the world again and, like a butterfly emerging from a kind of literary cocoon, she escaped from Mr. Porteous' teaching and books into the sunshine of calls on acquaintances and drives in the Park.

Her first surprise on emerging from her seclusion was to find that Sally Byles had "an understanding" with Mr. Deighton and that the engagement was about to be announced.

Sally had emerged from her puppy fat and was now a slim, pretty debutante, radiant with happiness. To Sally, Perry Deighton was her shining knight in armor and all she seemed to want to do was to talk about his manifold merits by the hour. Jennie was at first amused, wondering how anyone as spirited as Sally could love the prim and censorious Mr. Deighton. Then she began to feel qualms of jealousy. Since the death of her grandparents, her husband had been urbane and polite but had refrained from any of those kisses and caresses which had disturbed her so much.

She was returning from a visit to Sally and was being helped from her carriage by a footman when, with a leaping of her senses, she saw the slim, debonair figure of her cousin, Guy, bearing down on her.

"Oh, Guy, how I have neglected you," cried Jennie, immediately contrite.

"How *slim* you are," smiled Guy, feeling his sun shine again. Jennie was very obviously not expecting a Charrington heir. He decided not to tell her that he had been refused admission to her home for fear she might have changed and would not wish to offend her husband. But ascertaining that Chemmy was from home, he let Jennie bring him into the drawing room and listened with disbelieving amazement to her tale of her months of mourning for her grandparents. And who shall blame Mr. Chalmers for his cynicism? No one really knows for sure the thoughts or emotions of another and, therefore, one credits other persons with one's own faults, beliefs and humors — particularly one's faults.

Guy made sympathetic noises while he privately felt a growing admiration for Jennie. What a little actress!

"I believe I shall see you at the Tremayne *musicale* this evening," said Guy, proud to have secured such an irreproachable invitation for himself.

Jennie nodded. "It will be my first party since . . . since . . ." her voice faltered.

Guy pressed her hand, thinking impatiently that she was overdoing her broken-hearted act a trifle.

Guy heard the sound of the Marquis returning and hastily took his leave. Chemmy, who was standing in the hall with Mr. Porteous, the tutor, gave him a civil nod, but the craggy Scotchman gave him a strange look from under his shaggy brows.

Jennie applied herself impatiently to her lessons for the rest of the afternoon. She found herself hoping that Guy would be *very* attentive to her that evening and that Chemmy would notice. Her husband sometimes did not even seem to notice she was a female!

The heavy brogue of her tutor broke into her thoughts. "I think, my leddy, that you have maistered a fair copperplate. We will finish today in this fashion. I will read you this passage from Cicero's *De amicitia* which you will write out for me. 'Nature ordains friendship with relatives, but it is never very stable.' Aye, just so."

The Tremayne's *musicale* was an elegant affair. Jennie was flushed and happy to be back at a party again. She looked very pretty in her half-mourning of lavender with touches of black. Guy was as attentive as she had hoped but her amiable husband smiled lazily on them both with unimpaired good humor.

A buffet supper was to be served in the conservatory after the recital and, as the chairs scraped back and people rose to their feet, Jennie noticed with a bitter little pang that Alice Waring was of the company.

Mrs. Waring was dressed in lavender also, but clinging and revealing lavender muslin, which seemed to mock Jennie's sedate half-mourning.

A magnificent collar of diamonds flashed on her creamy neck and a fairy-tale tiara of diamonds flashed in the gold of her hair. The Marquis had crossed to her side and was bending his head towards her, laughing at something she was saying.

Jennie became aware that Guy was studying the conflicting emotions on her face and said hurriedly, "What magnificent diamonds Mrs. Waring has on. I wonder if the Charrington diamonds are half as beautiful. Chemmy must have forgotten to give them to me. I must remind him."

Guy had such a sudden, brilliant, dazzling idea that he nearly choked. Hurriedly composing himself, he said in a low, sad voice, "I wouldn't do that if I were you, Jennie."

"Why?" demanded Jennie, her eyes wide with amazement.

"Oh, my wicked tongue," said Guy. "Never mind."

Jennie looked from Guy to the diamonds decorating Alice Waring and back to Guy again.

"If you do not tell me what you were about to say, I shall *never* speak to you again," retorted Jennie, her voice with a shrill edge.

"Hush, now. Forget it."

"Tell me," hissed Jennie. "Tell me, *now*."

"My dear," said Guy with a great show of reluctance, "I will only tell you what I know if you promise *never* to tell your husband. I do not wish to be killed."

"I'll promise you *anything*," said Jennie, stamping her foot.

"Very well," sighed Guy. "If you must know, the diamonds . . ."

"Come. Let me escort you to supper, dear heart," came the voice of the Marquis. Guy hurriedly retreated.

Jennie did not know what she ate, she did not know what Chemmy said. She picked at the food on her plate and gulped down a great quantity of wine and watched and watched for some opportunity to talk to Guy again.

To her horror, she heard the Marquis suggesting that they take their leave. Other guests were already departing. The Marquis turned his head to greet a friend and Jennie seized her opportunity. Muttering something about needing to repair her dress, she fled from the room, throwing Guy a pleading glance as she went. She ran lightly up the stairs and then paused half way and looked down into the hall until she saw Guy emerging from the conservatory.

"Well?" she whispered urgently. "Well?"

And Guy's mocking whisper floated back up the stairs, "The diamonds Alice is wearing *are* the Charrington diamonds."

The conservatory doors swung open behind him and a rush of noise poured into the hall as the Marquis and several other guests appeared.

Jennie went slowly and numbly down to join her husband. Silently, she listened to his pleasant drawl as they jolted home in the carriage. Silently, she sat in the drawing room with him, lifting the mixing bowls and cannisters out of the rosewood teapoy, preparatory to making the nightly pot of tea which they had become accustomed to sharing.

"You are very sad and worried-looking tonight," said the Marquis in a more serious voice than he normally used. "I had hoped your distress over your grandparents' death would have abated by now."

Jennie's numbness fled leaving her shaking from a series of violent emotions — jealousy, fear, loneliness, and hate for this two-faced thing of a husband who had just turned out not to be the paragon she had come to believe.

"I'll tell you why I'm sad," she said in a light voice which belied the violence of her feelings. "I haven't *really* been mourning for poor grandpapa. I have been mourning for myself."

She flashed a glittering smile in the direction of her large husband and then proceeded to pour tea with a steady hand.

"Yes, indeed," she went on, "if only the old man had died sooner, then I would have had money enough and not have had to endure this farce of a marriage."

"You're drunk," said her husband.

"In vino veritas," mocked his wife.

Jennie had often in the past hoped to provoke some violent reaction in her husband. She looked up into his eyes and realized she had succeeded beyond her wildest dreams.

He was standing over her, staring down at her with his blue eyes burning with rage.

"Get to your feet, madam," he said in a very gentle voice. "I married you for an heir and we shall do something about begetting one tonight for, by God, by tomorrow, the sight of you will make me impotent."

Jennie shook with fear and stared pleadingly up at him. She longed to hurl the story of the Charrington diamonds in his face, but she had given Guy her word, and for all her spoiled and willful behavior, Jennie was still the soul of honor.

"*Please,* Chemmy . . ." she began.

He picked her up in his arms, ignoring her cries and pleas and struggles and carried her upstairs to her bedroom.

He threw her on the bed and held her down by the simple expedient of grasping her neck in his long fingers and forcing her head back on the pillows. Deaf to her broken sobs and cries, he stripped her naked with the other hand, the loose and flimsy styles of the day making it all too easy.

"This is rape," she gasped.

"It will not be," he said grimly, sinking on to

the bed beside her.

He began to kiss her fiercely and passionately from the top of her head to the soles of her feet and only when she finally lay trembling and un-resisting in his arms, did he remove his own clothes.

At one point before dawn, she turned in his arms and laid her head on his broad chest and fell quietly and peacefully asleep like a very young child.

The Marquis of Charrington lay very still in the gray light and stared down at the top of her curls. He then stared at the curling Chinese dragons on the bed hangings and wondered how he could possibly have been such a fool. He had, despite his protests to the contrary, fallen in love at first sight. He had given his heart and his name to what he had thought was an endearing, willful child. But the child had shown herself to be the type of woman with which he was all too familiar, hard and grasping with a bank ledger instead of a heart. He had put down her passion for her cousin to nothing more than a girlish crush which she would easily outgrow. But they were well-matched, Jennie and Guy. His little child-bride had only married him for his money. Had she been able to get her hands on her grand-father's fortune before the wedding, she would have laughed in his face.

Though he was bitter and disappointed, it did not strike him as odd that he, who had prided himself on loyalty, could trust and believe in someone, then later believe that this someone was everything that was cheap and conniving.

The fact was that the small ember of jealousy for Guy had suddenly burst into a roaring flame and he would have seized on anything at that moment to show that Jennie was not worthy of his love.

He had been feted and petted and sought after for so long because of his wealth and his title. He believed Jennie to be no better than the rest. To date, the Marquis had had a pleasant life paying for his pleasures. Now he was paying for them, not in gold, but in humiliation and rage.

But she looked so small and defenseless, lying beside him on the large bed. He felt a momentary pang as he thought of her beauty, her youth and her many endearing ways. His mind closed down like a steel trap on these soft thoughts as being the mawkish weakness of a fool.

He was not surprised at her passionate response of the night. He was expert enough to arouse genuine passion in the bosom of even the most hardened courtesan. That rare and magic gift of love was not to be his. He wished he had never touched her.

He would never touch her again.

Chapter Eight

Sunlight blazed down on the dusty streets of London. It was another perfect summer's day.

Jennie slowly awoke and immediately turned to the other side of the bed, but her husband had gone.

She smiled lazily to herself. What a fool she had been. She was in love with her husband, had been in love with him all along.

She became aware that someone was moving about the room and sat up in bed, clutching the covers to her neck. A prim elderly lady in a print dress had emerged from the dressing room with an armful of clothes over her arm, which she proceeded to lay out on a day bed by the window.

Seeing Jennie awake, the retainer dropped a low curtsey. "I am Jeffries, my lady," she said. "Your ladyship's new lady's maid."

She bustled forward with the bed tray containing Jennie's chocolate. Jennie looked up at her new maid's severe, wrinkled face and thought pettishly that her husband might at least have consulted her wishes before employing the woman. She would have preferred someone much younger and much prettier.

Then something about the maid's name struck her as being familiar.

"Jeffries," she murmured. "Now, where have I heard that name before?"

"My brother it was, ma'am," said the maid. "He was dear Lord Charles' footman and, when he died, your dear lord — your husband — he calls on me finding out somehow as how I had been retired from my previous employ and he offers me a good pension. Well, I was taken aback but I told him that I would not feel right taking the money without working for it and he said as how his lady wife was looking for a lady's maid."

Jennie bit her lip in vexation. She had not yet mastered enough worldly poise to muster up the courage to apologize to a servant and therefore felt doubly guilty. How on earth could she have forgotten poor old Jeffries! But her eyes filled with tears and that was enough mark of respect for the lady's maid who said quickly, "There is no need for you to upset yourself, my lady. My brother enjoyed his life and he was indeed very old when he died. And he would have liked to die in harness, so to speak."

Jennie climbed out of bed and allowed Jeffries to help her into a pretty morning gown of figured lilac silk.

Her hair was cleverly combed into artistic disarray and she looked at her image in the mirror with pleased satisfaction. "You have done wonders, Jeffries," she said warmly. Much as she longed to rush to her husband's arms, a slightly more mature Jennie curbed her impatience and asked the lady's maid many questions about her welfare and told her that the rest of the old servants were well looked after at Charrington Court, but pined for Runbury Manor, which they still looked on as home.

"I thought I should perhaps sell the property," said Jennie, half to herself, "but my husband will not hear of it and already has a steward in residence to supervise repairs to the building and to the tenants' property."

"Oh, his lordship would *never* sell Runbury, my lady," exclaimed Jeffries. " 'Tis a good sound property and he will be wanting it for his heirs."

The thought of heirs and of how pleasurable it was to go about begetting them made Jennie blush rosily and hasten from the room, no longer able to check her impatience to see her husband.

To her disappointment, Chemmy was dressed to go out and was standing by the street door talking to Roberts, the butler.

She paused to admire him, wondering how she could ever have possibly found him foppish. His curly brimmed beaver was perched on his golden hair and his great height set off his magnificent coat of Bath superfine to perfection.

Then his light pleasant drawl carried to her ears with dreadful clarity.

"Very well, Roberts," the Marquis was saying, "I think you understand my instructions. Mr. Guy Chalmers is to be admitted at all times."

Jennie stared in amazement. Then she gave herself a mental shake. Of course! Chemmy had no longer any reason to be jealous of Guy after last night.

With a smile on her lips, she ran lightly down the rest of the stairs, crying, "Where are you going so early, my love?"

The Marquis turned very slowly and looked at her over the head of his butler. Gone was the sleepy, teasing amiability. His eyes were as cold as the winter sea.

"Good morning, madam," he said with bone-chilling formality. "I did not expect your presence so early but perhaps it is just as well. Pray step into the morning room, madam. I would have a few words with you."

Nervous and silent, Jennie walked past him into the room as he held open the door. He followed her in and politely drew forward a chair for her.

"Please, Chemmy . . ." began Jennie, beginning to plead for she knew not what.

"The time has come for us to put our cards on the table, madam," said Chemmy, still standing.

"You have made it perfectly clear that you married me for my money. Had your grandfather died in time, you would have had no need of it. You have also gone to considerable lengths to try to start an affair with Guy Chalmers and I, in turn, believing you to be only guilty of an immature infatuation, went to considerable lengths to see that it did not happen.

"I believed you to be a young lady of good breeding, of heart. This seemed to me to be borne out by your evidently real grief after the death of your grandparents. But even this was a sham. So I took revenge on you, but it turned against me and I feel even more sick and bitter now than I did last night. Ours shall be the marriage of convenience you wished. You will, however, keep your affairs well away from polite society or I shall seek a divorce. Come, my dear, smile and be happy! You have what you wanted."

Overcome by fear, Jennie broke her promise to Guy. "What about the Charrington diamonds?" she cried.

Chemmy looked at her in utter contempt.

"Come with me," he said abruptly. He strode from the room and Jennie walked after him, feeling as if she were moving in a nightmare.

He marched up the stairs and along to his bedroom, opening the door and propelling Jennie into the room.

He walked to a strong box in the corner, took some keys from his pocket and, after examining them carefully, selected one, inserted it in the lock and then threw open the lid. His long fingers scrabbled among cases and boxes and then he turned around, a tiara in one hand and a necklace in the other.

While Jennie stood, rigid with shock, he walked forward and gently placed the tiara on her hair and clasped the ice cold weight of the necklace around her neck and then stood back and surveyed his handiwork.

"There you are," he said. "Now you have *everything* you want."

He marched out, leaving Jennie, still standing, the diamonds flashing and blazing and burning in her hair and on her breast.

Far away downstairs, the street door banged — far away in another country of warmth and laugher and normality. She could hear her husband calling to John, the groom, then the rattle of carriage wheels and the sound of horses hooves moving off over the cobbles.

How long she stood there, she did now know. After some time, she became aware that the butler was standing framed in the doorway. He showed no surprise at being confronted by the glittering spectacle that was Jennie. "Mr. Chalmers awaits you below, my lady," he said in a colorless voice.

Jennie started. She must see Guy. She must have Guy's permission to tell Chemmy that it was he, Guy, who had told her the Charrington diamonds had been given to Alice Waring and that she had been subsequently jealous. Chemmy now obviously thought she had demanded the diamonds out of greed.

She raised her shaking hands and removed the tiara and necklace and handed them to the butler. "Please keep these safe, Roberts, until my husband returns," said Jennie. "I do not wish to see them again."

"Very good, my lady," said Roberts woodenly. Then he seemed to notice for the first time the pinched and drawn look on Jennie's face.

"Shall I tell Mr. Chalmers you are not at home, my lady?" he asked.

"Oh . . . oh, no," said Jennie. "I *must* see him."

"Certainly, my lady," said Roberts, his mouth drawing in slightly at the corners.

Guy was lounging in the drawing room when Jennie burst in. He jumped to his feet and flung his arms around her. "Jennie! You look more ravishing than ever," said Guy.

Jennie quietly disengaged herself from his embrace and looked intensely up into his eyes. "Guy," she said slowly, "the diamonds that Alice was wearing were *not* the Charrington diamonds. I must have your permission to tell Chemmy how the misunderstanding came about."

"Well, you can't," said Guy, looking everywhere but into her eyes. "You gave me your word. *I* can't help it if some malicious gossip misled me. I didn't want to tell you in the first place but you wouldn't leave me alone. You silly goose! What happened?"

Leaving out her experience of the night, Jennie told him the rest, word for word. "So you see," she finished miserably. "I *must* tell Chemmy. He believes me to be mercenary."

"What about *me?*" asked Guy. "We can be together now. That butler let me in for the first time."

"Do you mean to say he used to *refuse* you permission. Oooooh! Now Chemmy doesn't care *what* I do."

133

"Well, that's all to the good," said Guy in a caressing voice. He tried to draw her into his arms again but she shrank away.

"D-don't, Guy," stammered Jennie. "I know now I don't feel *that* for you. I am exceedingly fond of you . . . as a brother . . . no more. I-I l-love my husband."

"Miss Byles," said Roberts from the doorway.

"Gad's 'oonds!" swore Guy to himself as Jennie pinned a smile of welcome on her face. "I must do something quickly or the countryside will soon be crawling with little Charringtons. That's the trouble with these healthy country girls, they breed like damned rabbits."

Aloud, he said, "I must take my leave, Jennie. Your servant, Miss Byles."

Sally watched his retreating back. "I never did like Guy Chalmers," she said as soon as that young man was out of earshot. "He's all smiles on the outside and I think he's rotten in the inside. Just like a whited sulphurator."

"Not sulphurator," corrected Jennie. "Sepulchre."

"Oh," said Sally, much disappointed. "I thought it was sulphurator. You know, because of sulphur being sort of hellish and going with brimstone and all that. Sepulchre, dear me, *not* the same. But then, our Bishop speaks so quietly, 'tis hard to make out the words. Oh, Jennie, I do so need your advice, and not about whited sulphurators either!"

Jennie tried to banish her own troubles to the

back of her mind. Perhaps if she concentrated on Sally's, she could forget a little of her own.

"It's about Perry," burst out Sally. "I *can't* marry him!"

"Why?" Jennie stared at her friend in dismay.

"It's clothes, clothes, clothes," wailed Sally. "Perry says I have *no* taste and says he will choose my trousseau. What do you think of this dress?"

Sally was wearing a modish walking gown of flaming scarlet taffeta. The color was perhaps a little daring, but it had a demurely high neckline with a little starched Elizabethan frill of lace and the bodice was intricately tucked. It made Sally's slightly sallow skin look golden and was complimented by the intense blue color of her eyes. Her brown ringlets were neatly arranged under a fetching poke bonnet and, in all, she looked as if she had stepped from the pages of *La Belle Assemblée*.

"I think you look very fine," said Jennie wonderingly.

"Well, Perry says my taste in colors is *fast*," said Sally, her eyes filling with tears. "And . . . and he says that when we are married, I must wear *nothing* but pastels. He-he is even going to choose the *more intimate* items of apparel and suggested I buy a stock of *flannel* nightgowns since flannel prevents the ague and silk and satin in the bedchamber are only suitable for a member of the Fashionable Impure. And . . . and . . . oh! . . . there is *worse!*"

"There is?" said Jennie weakly.

"Yes. My parents allow us some time together since we are to be married after all. And Perry was wont to kiss me a lot and it was so very exciting and I began to kiss him back, *so* passionately, and he d-drew a-way f-from m-me in in-horror and s-said, 'Madam, wh-what d-do you think y-you are *doing?*' and I feel *awful!*" ended Sally, collapsing into a burst of noisy tears.

Jennie gently untied the strings of her friend's bonnet, took it off and laid it on the sofa. Then she held a vinaigrette under Sally's nose and said helplessly, "There, there. Don't take on so. I am sure you refine too much on it," and all the while her mind was remembering Chemmy as she had first seen him at Runbury Manor, when he had held the vinaigrette under his nose and she had called him a fop.

"How can I help?" she asked, after Sally had at last composed herself.

"I thought perhaps you could ask Chemmy for advice," said Sally. "Perhaps he could talk to Perry for me."

"I'm afraid I can't," said Jennie. "Chemmy *hates* m-me and th-thinks I m-married him for his money." She burst into tears. Sally burst into sympathetic tears as well and the two girls hugged each other and cried their eyes out.

Their feelings somewhat relieved, they were finally able to drink some tea and Sally heard the whole story of Jennie's misunderstanding with Chemmy.

"It's Guy, that's who it is," said Sally. "*He's* the one who is jealous, mark my words. He's out to make trouble."

But Jennie would still not hear a word against Guy. He had been thoughtless in repeating malicious gossip, nothing more.

"Mr. Porteous, your tutor, is here," said Roberts, suddenly appearing.

"A tutor!" cried Sally. "Never say you are turned bluestocking, Jennie?"

But Jennie felt she had divulged enough secrets for the morning and did not want to tell her friend that a tutor had been employed to teach her to read and write. Although Jennie had long since mastered both these skills, the clever Mr. Porteous had given her a thirst for knowledge and Jennie had remained interested in the business of expanding the horizons of her mind and Mr. Porteous had remained employed.

"Show him in, Roberts," said Jennie. "I think I shall forego my lessons today, Sally. Perhaps we could go for a walk in this beautiful sunshine. Ah, Mr. Porteous. Sally, allow me to present my tutor, Mr. Porteous. Mr. Porteous, Miss Byles."

To Jennie's surprise, the tutor bent over Sally's hand with some elegance. "I am charmed," said Mr. Porteous, "to meet such a young and pretty leddy with such an eye for the fashion. I may be a crusty old dominie, Miss Byles, but I pride myself on having a good eye for color."

Sally blushed and flashed a triumphant look at Jennie from under her lashes.

"Tell me, Mr. Porteous," said Sally dimpling up at him. "Would you say that a gentleman should have the right to dictate to his wife on the matter of fashion?"

Mr. Porteous' shaggy brows drew together as he appeared to give the matter great thought. "Weel, no, Miss Byles," he said after a long silence. "Provided one has enough money, clothes are, I would say, an extension of one's personality. Now if someone tries to change another's style of dress, he is saying, 'I am not content with you as you are. I do not love you for yourself. I only love you for what I think I can change you into.' I get a great enjoyment out of seeing a weel-dressed, pretty leddy, Miss Byles . . . such as yourself, for example . . . but in the way I would enjoy looking at a rare piece of porcelain or a fine chair. It appeals to ma *aesthetic* senses."

"But if you were in *love?*" demanded Sally intensely, while Jennie gazed from one to the other in amazement.

"Aye, then, that's another matter," said Mr. Porteous. "I doubt if I would *see* the clothes, or the eyes, or the lips or the hair. I would simply see someone who would make the sun rise for me when she entered the room and bring down the black night when she left. Aye, just so."

Jennie began to feel uncomfortable. She coughed gently to get Sally's attention.

"Sally . . . if we are to go for that walk, we had best get started now," she said.

"No lessons, my leddy?" queried Mr. Porteous.

"No lessons today," smiled Jennie, despite the lump of ice in her stomach.

"I shall not keep you, then," said the tutor wistfully. "I take a few dauners through the Park myself from time to time but I have not much of an acquaintance in London having but recently come to town. Aye, it is not quite the same to be out in the flowers and the sunshine on one's own."

"Then you shall walk with us!" cried Sally, while Jennie stared at her friend in dismay. What a conniving old devil Mr. Porteous was turning out to be! But urged by her friend, she left to find her bonnet and shawl. Perhaps she might see her husband's tall figure. She could no longer wait until he came home. Damn Guy! Her happiness was at stake and she would *not* keep her word. And Chemmy would smile on her again with that seductive sleepy amiability and she would feel his arms holding her once more. Having come to this decision, it was a considerably more cheerful Jennie who set out into the sunshine with Sally and Mr. Porteous.

Mr. Porteous turned out to be a pleasant and informative companion and Sally had recovered her spirits, although Jennie was amazed at the *boldness* of her friend who seemed to be flirting in an extremely *fast* way with the tutor.

They spent much longer on their walk than they had intended and Jennie became suddenly anxious to return home quickly in case Chemmy was there.

Mr. Porteous suggested they could take a shortcut through Vole Lane and so save some time and, after some hesitation, the ladies agreed. No one ever knew quite how Vole Lane had managed to survive in all its sinister dirt and squalor among the stately streets and squares of the fashionable West End. It was short and dark and smelly, with crowded old tenements leaning drunkenly on either side. It was thankfully deserted and the ladies hurried along, holding their skirts high out of the mud which always seemed to infest Vole Lane, no matter how hot the summer.

There was a furtive scurrying sound behind them as Mr. Porteous swung around. No one. At the far end of the lane, the trees of the Park swayed and turned in the lightest of summer breezes, making the Park look like an Eden shining at the end of some particularly noisome alleyway out of hell.

Mr. Porteous walked along uneasily.

There was a sudden loud clatter of running feet. Holding his cane he swung around. With the lightning speed of the ferret he resembled, a little, red-eyed man tried to nip under Mr. Porteous' arm and drive the long wicked looking knife he held in his hand straight into Jennie's ribs.

Mr. Porteous brought his cane down with a savage blow on the man's wrist and the knife spun off into the kennel.

Jennie's assailant staggered, regaining his balance and turned to flee. With surprising agility, Mr. Porteous caught him by the back of the neck and began to shake him like a rat.

"The Runners will be glad to get a look at you, laddie," he grated.

The little man squirmed in his grasp. "I was paid to do it, guv," he panted. "Let me go an' I'll tell you. I swear. You're hurting me!"

"All right, you scum, who paid you?" demanded Mr. Porteous while Jennie and Sally clutched each other for support.

" 'Twas 'er husband," gasped the man. "God's word, it was."

"Fustian!" said Mr. Porteous. "You do not even know the name of this leddy."

"That I do," said the man, turning his small red-rimmed eyes towards Jennie. "The Marquis of Charrington paid me and that there's his rib, his wife, that's wot."

Mr. Porteous swore in amazement, slackened his grip and the assailant saw his chance and took it. He lashed out a vicious kick, which caught Mr. Porteous full in the stomach and then he fled, disappearing into the blackness of the lane.

Sally helped Mr. Porteous who had fallen to his knees.

But Jennie stood still. The horrible rat-faced man's words seemed to pound and pound in her ears:

"The Marquis of Charrington paid me . . ."

141

Chapter Nine

Chemmy paused on the threshold of the drawing room with Perry behind him, his eyebrows lifting at the strange scene that met his eyes.

Mr. Porteous was lying stretched out on the sofa while Sally was perched on the edge of it, trying to persuade him to drink a glass of wine. His wife was standing a little way away at the fireplace, looking white and frightened.

Perry was the first to speak. "Miss Byles," he said sternly, "you are practically sitting in that man's lap. Get up immediately."

Sally got to her feet with a mulish expression on her face.

"I was administering to Mr. Porteous," she said, tossing her ringlets. "He was hurt saving Jennie's life!"

"I would have a word with you in private, my lord," said Mr. Porteous, weakly raising his head.

"Very well," said Chemmy. "Perry, please take Miss Byles home. And madam" — to Jennie — "wait for me in the morning room."

Sally looked as if she was about to refuse to go, but an appealing look from Jennie sped her on her way.

When they were alone, the Marquis noticed that Mr. Porteous abandoned his role of invalid

142

and sat up on the sofa, looking very alert and businesslike.

"It seems I am in your debt," said the Marquis. "Pray, tell me what happened."

Mr. Porteous slowly and concisely explained the details of the attack, ending with the man's strange accusation.

The Marquis sat very still, studying the ends of his fingernails.

"Very strange," he said at last. "And did any of you believe that I had hired someone to kill my wife?"

"My lord," cried Mr. Porteous, springing to his feet. "As if any of us *would*."

"You are a very useful man to have around, Porteous," said the Marquis. "I am very grateful to you. Which puts me in mind of something else. I have been considering employing a secretary and I feel you would be the very man for the job. I would like you to live here if that is convenient."

"Thank you, my lord," said Mr. Porteous. "*Very* convenient."

"You will, of course, continue to tutor my wife. I would also like you to keep an eye on her, Mr. Porteous. Make her your friend. Perhaps there are some things about my wife I do not understand. I will be frank with you, since I know you to be a man of honor. I believe my wife married me for my money, but there is yet in my mind a nagging seed of doubt."

"There bluidy well should be," shouted Mr.

Porteous. "My lady us nothing mair than an art-less child."

"Dear me," said the Marquis softly. "The democracy of the Scots. Remember your place, my good man."

"I will not apologize for my loyalty to her ladyship," said Mr. Porteous, standing his ground. "Miss Byles is a friend of my leddy and anyone who has Miss Byles as a friend is nigh on the road to paradise!"

The Marquis blinked in astonishment. Then he understood what had overset the tutor's nerves and what also had made him lie so weakly on the sofa so long as Sally was in the room.

"What a busy day you have had to be sure," murmured the Marquis lazily. "You save my wife's life and fall in love with her best friend and all in the space of a few hours!"

All the fight went out of the tutor and he stood and hung his head like an overgrown schoolboy. "Ye think I'm cheeky, my lord, and ye would be right. But I maun speak what is in my heart. I cannae thole deception," he said, his brogue at its thickest.

"In that case," said the Marquis, "you will be an excellent secretary. But do not expect me to smile on your passion for Miss Byles. She is, after all, about to marry *my* closest friend."

"Aye, just so. I'm old enough to be her faither anyway," said the tutor with a heavy sigh.

"Courage, man! How old are you, Porteous?"

"Forty-one, my lord."

"A mere child, I assure you," said the Marquis, ringing the bell. "Ah, Roberts. Have Mr. Porteous conveyed to his lodgings in my carriage and then send my wife to me."

"My lord."

"Yes, Roberts?"

"My lady gave me the diamonds for safe-keeping until you return. She does not wish to see them again."

"Very well, Roberts," said Chemmy. "Have them conveyed to my room."

When the doors had closed behind the butler and Mr. Porteous, Chemmy walked over to a little desk at the window and picked up a long, thin stilleto which he used for cutting the pages of new books and turned it idly over and over in his fingers while he waited for his wife.

He wondered why she was returning the diamonds and decided it was simply a childish trick to impress him and, at the same time, humiliate him further. In Jennie's spoiled child naïveté, he thought he saw the workings of a cold and acquisitive brain. Perhaps she had even hired someone to pretend to try to kill her and throw the blame for it onto him as part of some devious plan. Damn her!

With absolute clarity, he suddenly remembered the silken feel of her skin against his naked body. Suddenly his carefully cultivated mask of urbanity cracked and shattered and, beside himself with longing, anguish and rage, he stabbed the long knife again and again into the soft leather top of the desk.

A sharp noise made him turn. Jennie stood watching him, the pupils of her eyes dilated with fear.

Hardly knowing what he was saying, he swept her a bow. "I do not *need* you this evening," he drawled. "I have a call to make on Mrs. Waring."

He pushed past her and a second later she heard the street door bang. She felt numb with terror. Her husband was a maniac — and a maniac hell-bent on killing her and marrying Alice Waring.

Jennie could not bear the thought of waiting alone in the house. She sent a footman to find her a chair to take her to Sally's home a few streets away.

Sally was fortunately at home. It transpired that she had been invited to a party that evening but Perry had been too angry with her to escort her. When Jennie was announced, Sally was sitting in the drawing room with her parents, the Honorable Mr. and Mrs. Augustus Byles, a jolly, plump, good-natured couple.

Mrs. Byles hailed Jennie's arrival with relief. "I am right glad you are come, Jennie," she said, rising and shaking out her skirts. "Mr. Byles and I are invited to an evening of cards but we did not want to leave Sally alone. Perhaps you can stay for some while and keep her company? You will? Splendid! Come, Mr. Byles. I declare I am anxious to be off. Such an irritating evening! As if I did not know how to behave like a parent after all these years. How *dare* he!"

"Perry," explained Sally gloomily, when her parents had left. "Not content with accusing me of philandering with servants . . . he meant Mr. Porteous, of course . . . he went on to tell Mama and Papa that I had been very badly brought up and so they were quite incensed with him as well, and I hoped against hope that Mama would tell me to give him his marching orders. But, no! She forgave him. Said that jealous men were always twitty.

"But, Jennie, enough of my worries. What about *yours?* You look terrified to death!"

"I am," said Jennie, and began to pour out the story of Chemmy's assault upon the desk, large tears beginning to roll down her face. "And *then* he said he was going to Mrs. Waring," she ended, taking an inadequate handkerchief out of her reticule and trying to mop her face with it.

"You must compose yourself, Jennie," said Sally in a muffled voice. "We shall drink a glass of Papa's madeira wine and you will feel more the thing. Oh! It-it's so *funny.*" And with that, the mirth that Sally had been trying to restrain poured out as she rolled around on the sofa and whooped and hiccupped.

"You've gone mad," snapped Jennie, anger drying her tears.

"It's not that," said Sally when she could. "I'm sorry to laugh but, poor Chemmy, he sounds so like Papa."

"What can a raving madman have in common

with Mr. Byles?" demanded Jennie angrily, comparing the mental picture of her husband stabbing at the desk with one of the usually cheerful and placid Mr. Byles.

"It's true," choked Sally, beginning to laugh again. "It's all right, Jennie. Don't glare at me like that. I'll explain.

"Well, we had in our employ in town a simply exquisite footman . . . like a young Adonis. Now, it was on that very gusty, blowy day about a se'enight ago and the wind was roaring down all the chimneys and Mama got a cinder in her eye and it was *terribly* painful.

"This footman . . . Bryant . . . happened to be in the room at the time, lighting the candles, you know, and he rushed forward with a handkerchief and offered to take the cinder from Mama's eye. Well, Mama was so grateful, she simply *clutched* on to him while Bryant worked away with a pocket handkerchief to get the cinder out.

"Papa errupted over the threshold. 'Damn, woman,' he roars, 'is this what goes on in mine household when I am abroad?' Poor Bryant *flees*. Mama tries to explain but Papa is so mad with jealousy, he won't listen.

"He throws all her pretty figurines from the mantle onto the floor and he starts jumping up and down on them . . . quite beside himself with rage, my dear . . . grinding them to a powder and shouting, 'There, madam, there! What d'ye think of that. Heh? Heh?' *Quite* mad, I assure you. But Papa would never *kill* Mama, you know.

In fact he bought her a very pretty trinket. He even apologized to Bryant . . . not that it stopped him from sending Bryant to our house in the country, for Papa said that a young man like that around the house was simply *throwing* temptation in any female's way."

"And you think . . ." began Jennie, wonderingly.

"I don't think . . . I *know*," said Sally triumphantly. "Imagine for a minute that there had *not* been an attempt on your life and you had found Chemmy behaving like that. You would have simply thought he had the gout or had lost money on the Funds or something . . ."

"Perhaps," said Jennie slowly. "But Chemmy is . . . well . . . always so *mannered* . . . so very much the gentleman . . ."

"So is my Papa," pointed out Sally reasonably. "At least, most days of the week, that is. Now, I wouldn't mind if Perry would go off his head once in a while instead of sitting with his cane stuffed in his mouth, emanating an atmosphere of disapproval, or occasionally unstoppering himself to tell me my dresses are fast or that I'm making sheep's eyes at Mr. Porteous . . . which, of course, I *am*. Isn't he *gorgeous*, Jennie. So silent and masterful. When he looks at me from under those dear shaggy eyebrows and says, 'Aye, just so,' I go quite weak at the knees."

"Sally," exclaimed Jennie. "It would never answer, you know. Your parents would never hear of it."

"Not in the ordinary way, they wouldn't," grinned Sally. "Give them a little more of dear Mr. Deighton and they'd give their blessing to a tiger from Exeter 'Change!"

"He's rather old, isn't he?" said Jennie. "Mr. Porteous, I mean."

"Nonsense!" said Sally. "If you think Mr. Porteous is old, then Chemmy is *ancient*."

"Chemmy is thirty-five!"

"Exactly!"

Both girls glared at each other and then Jennie began to laugh. "Oh, Sally," she said. "You are better than a tonic. Somehow life seems normal again."

"Good," grinned Sally. "And why should you be amazed and frightened if Chemmy throws a tantrum? Do you still hold your breath?"

"Oh, dear," blushed Jennie. "I haven't done *that* for a long time. What a spoiled brat I must have been. And how on earth could I be so spoiled? Grandmama and Grandpapa were quite strict with me, you know."

"Guy was the one who spoiled you," said Sally. "I don't like that young man."

"Guy *loves* me, like a sister," said Jennie, flying to her cousin's defense and then guiltily remembered his anything-but-brotherly kisses. "I must talk to Chemmy tonight and explain everything."

"I wouldn't do that. I would leave him to cool off," said the worldly-wise Sally. "Why don't you go away somewhere and leave him alone so that he'll miss you. He'll never see things in perspective with you underfoot. Tell him that you want to see the improvements to your old home. You told me the servants . . . the old ones . . . are at Charrington Court. Have them conveyed back again, order new furniture, get the old place cleaned out. With all that, you will not have time to mope. And I shall come and visit you."

"Very well," said Jennie. "But I shall say *something* to Chemmy. I cannot bear him to go on thinking me mercenary."

"Give Mr. Porteous a goodnight kiss for me," grinned Sally. "Has he moved in?"

"I don't know," said Jennie, "and furthermore you *must* tell Perry you are not going to marry him, especially if you are dreaming about someone else. Has it ever dawned on you, Sally, that Perry might be in love with you?"

"Pooh!" said Sally. "That one only loves himself!"

"Perry, if the girl is making you so unhappy, why marry her?" demanded the Marquis of Charrington.

He and Mr. Deighton had spent a long, dreary and silent evening playing cards. Both of them had been reluctant to return to their respective homes and, instead, had driven several miles out on the Brighton road, looking for a congenial hostelry where they could first clear their heads with the cool air of the drive and then revive their spirits with a good bottle of wine.

151

They had finally alighted at the Three Sisters Inn at Horley and had found themselves a quiet table in the small garden at the back.

The evening was very still and warm. A small moon rose high above and the smells of grass and flowers mingled with the homelier smells of ale, wine and coffee which drifted from the taproom.

Perry had burst into speech under the relaxing influence of a good bottle of port. He had entreated Chemmy to talk to the tutor and tell that presumptuous Highlander to keep his roving eyes on his books.

The Marquis had refused. He was in a difficult position, he said. The tutor had saved his wife's life and appeared to be receiving every encouragement from Sally. Also, the tutor had come with impeccable references from the Duke of Westerland, who had also written from his Scottish fastness to say that Mr. Porteous came from a very old family and that his bloodline was impeccable. The man had, in fact, everything to recommend him except money.

"How did the trouble with Sally start?" asked the Marquis, prepared to sink himself in Perry's troubles so that he might cease worrying about his own. He could not, after all, discuss his wife, even with his best friend. Discussing her with Porteous was a different matter. He needed Porteous as a watchdog.

"I did not like the way she dressed and told her that I would choose her trousseau for her," said Perry.

The Marquis groaned. "Perry, my dear Perry, if Miss Byles was in the habit of arraying herself in vulgar or ostentatious clothes I could see the point, but she is always very attractively gowned."

"That's just it," complained Perry. "She's too attractive by half. Who would have thought she would have changed from that plump little country miss? I see the way other men look at her and I can't stand it."

That was when the Marquis had pointed out that Perry might be better off not marrying Sally if she made him so unhappy.

"But I shall be even more unhappy without her," said Perry moodily. "I am also shocked at the intensity of my feelings. After all, one does not have passionate relationships with one's future wife."

The Marquis put down his glass and stared at his friend in amazement. "Why ever not?"

"Well, it's not *decent*, is it?" pleaded Perry. "One reserves that sort of behavior for the ladies of the town. And when Sally responded to me rather ardently, I had to rebuke her."

"You had to . . ." The Marquis groaned. "Look you, Perry. Women are the same creatures whether they come from the demimonde or from our world. They are human. They want passionate love as much as we do. If Sally ever wants to see you again, I shall be much surprised. How on earth did you come about these Gothic notions?"

"It was my father," said Perry. "He told me that respectable women were completely different from the other kind and that any woman who responded to me ardently would respond to any man ardently."

"Stuff!" said the Marquis. "I've never heard such rubbish. But why then did you lash out at Jennie and call her frigid?"

"That," said Perry primly, "was simply because she was not performing her marital duties."

"Oh, Perry, Perry. If it is not too late, I would make most violent love to Miss Sally the next time you see her."

"But that is lust!" exclaimed Perry.

"It would only be lust if you didn't love the girl. How can I have known you so long," said the Marquis, "and not have realized what a load of Methodist garbage was swimming around in that kennel you call a brain? No. Don't call me out. Someone has got to put you right. I shall do my best for you. If you like, I shall gently warn Mr. Porteous off but I cannot make him keep away from Miss Byles if Miss Byles is hell-bent on flirting with him."

Unaware that he was the subject of so much heart-searching, the tutor, Mr. Porteous, arrived at the Marquis' house early the next morning carrying a battered valise and anxious to start his duties as secretary.

He looked with satisfaction around the comfortable room assigned to him. He would make his fortune yet! He had long known that the road to advancement lay in the South.

Roberts showed him into the study and said that his lordship had left instructions that Mr. Porteous was to deal with the morning post. The newspapers had been ironed and taken up to his lordship and after his lordship had finished with them, it would then be Mr. Porteous' duty to clip out all articles pertaining to agriculture, in case his lordship might have missed anything. The estate books from the Marquis' various properties were being sent to him, said Roberts, so that Mr. Porteous could audit the accounts and suggest improvements.

Roberts retired, leaving Mr. Porteous to look proudly around his new domain. He tugged open the French window, which led out to the small garden at the back of the house, letting in the warm, scented morning air of summer. A blackbird sang from the opposite rooftop and the scent of roses and lime drifted into the room.

Mr. Porteous drew a chair up to a fine rococo pedestal desk and began to go through the correspondence.

Almost the first thing to catch his eye was a large heavy red seal on a long letter — a seal that was all too familiar.

With a suddenly thudding heart, he cracked open the seal and carefully spread out the thick parchment.

"My dear Charrington," he read, holding the letter in hands which had become damp and moist, "I trust you are still finding our good Porteous satisfactory. However, I must beg of you to send him back. My youngest boy, Ian, is about ready to start cramming for Eton and I know of no one else who would get the boy past the entrance exams like our man Porteous. He is a brilliant scholar and I am glad I was able to give him the opportunity of this working holiday in the metropolis, but I am worried about my son's education and, of course, Mrs. Porteous would be delighted to see her husband again. In fact, I have had to forceably restrain the good lady from making the journey to London. I fear our Porteous is a devil with the ladies! Congratulations and felicitations on your marriage. We would be delighted to entertain you on your next visit north. Yr. humble and obedient servant, Westerland."

Mr. Porteous stared at the letter while the bird outside sang on and a little errant breeze gently moved the heavy heads of the roses. There was the sound of movements upstairs and then the sound of someone descending the staircase.

With a shaking hand, Mr. Porteous lit the corner of the letter and threw it into the fireplace.

Just in time! A minute later, the door opened and the Marquis strolled in. Mr. Porteous rose and bowed, and then turned and sat down again, bending his head over his work. He did not see how curiously Chemmy was staring at the wisp of smoke in the fireplace or how intently he was staring at the small red pool of sealing wax which was dripping slowly from the andirons.

But the Marquis only said, "I am going out, Porteous. There is a prime Arab mare on sale at Tattersall's and I am anxious to purchase it for my wife. Do not tell her. I wish it to be a surprise."

Mr. Porteous rose and bowed without looking fully at the Marquis.

"Oh, just one other thing, Porteous," said the Marquis. "I do not wish you to encourage the attentions of Miss Byles. You do understand?"

"Yes, my lord," said the tutor in a grim voice, staring at the floor.

Chemmy left in a thoughtful mood. His secretary had just burned a letter and he, Chemmy, was very interested to find out what letter it had been.

But first, the horse. He was anxious to study his wife's reaction to the present.

He returned some two hours later, pleased with his purchase and furious with his company.

Guy Chalmers had joined him at Tattersall's and had stuck to him like a leech, prattling on about the days when he and Jennie had gone riding. He had insisted on accompanying the Marquis home. Chemmy had noted the way Jennie's face lit up at the sight of Guy and had sent the horse to the stables, taking himself off to his private sitting room to indulge in something remarkably like a sulk.

His usual good nature reasserted itself, however, and he descended the stairs to look for his wife, only to find to his fury that his surprise present was a surprise no more. Mr. Chalmers, Roberts informed him with gloomy relish, had informed her ladyship of her new mount and her ladyship had gone to the Park.

"With Mr. Chalmers?" grated the Marquis.

"No, my lord," said Roberts, pleased at being able to impart some good news to his grim-faced master, "with John, your groom. Mr. Chalmers had a pressing engagement."

Not knowing that Guy had told Jennie he had left, Chemmy could only think that she was more interested in her present than in the giver and was as spoiled and avaricious as he had come to believe.

He sent Mr. Porteous on an errand and then went into the study to examine the hearth.

There was no ash in the hearth and the andirons had been scrubbed and polished until they gleamed like silver.

The Marquis stared at the fireplace, his brows drawn together. He suddenly thought it would be a very good idea if he wrote to the Duke of Westerland and asked His Grace to send the reply to his club.

Jennie was enchanted with her horse. It was the daintiest thing imaginable, with delicate mincing steps and a long silky mane. "What shall

I call her?" she asked John.

The groom put his head on one side and studied the prancing little horse. "The way she moves," he said, his face creasing in a rare smile, "puts me in mind of Mr. Garforth's Rosalind that won the Subscription Cup at Oxford."

"Then Rosalind it shall be," laughed Jennie, patting the mare's golden mane. Jennie felt as if she had just emerged from a nightmare. Chemmy must have some regard for her. No man who hated and disliked his wife would ever have bought her such a beautiful present. What a pity he had not been at home so that he could see her setting off. They could even have gone riding together.

The sun sparkled on the grass and, as it was not yet the fashionable hour, there were few people in the Park.

"Please, may I gallop, John? *Please*," begged Annie. "I know it is not the thing but there is hardly anyone around."

She looked so young and so pretty in her blue velvet riding habit that John grinned and nodded his head. "I'll have a bit of a gallop as well, my lady. Off you go!"

Instead of galloping along the cinder path, Jennie swung her mount over a long stretch of grass. The little mare sped like an arrow and Jennie laughed aloud with the sheer exhilaration of the sport. Suddenly the mare bucked and then reared violently.

Had Jennie been more aware, had she guessed

for a minute that she was about to be thrown and tensed her body, she might have broken her bones. But it seemed to her that one minute she was on her horse and then next, she was hitting the ground with a sickening thud.

John came racing up, dismounted and helped her to her feet. The little mare pranced away from them rolling its eyes, flecks of foam on its mouth.

"I'm all right," gasped Jennie. "See to Rosalind."

John managed at last to catch the horse by the reins and patted its nose and talked to it in a soothing monotone until it stood still. But it still trembled and rolled its eyes. John studied it for a minute and then bent down and unbuckled the girth and lifted off the saddle. A thin trickle of blood rolled down the mare's flanks.

John turned over the saddle and stared at it while Jennie came up and looked over his shoulder. A half inch of wicked-looking spike was sticking out of the saddle.

"An evil trick," muttered John. "This spike was so inserted into the saddle that it would eventually work through it and stab the animal in the back."

Jennie began to shake with fear. She had a sudden vision of Chemmy stabbing the desk, Chemmy who had bought her the horse and had immediately gone out instead of giving her the present himself.

"I could have been killed," she whispered.

"Maybe," said John. "His lordship had better hear about this."

He already knows, thought Jennie.

Chemmy heard the tale of the spike and, after John had been dismissed, he turned to his wife. "There is only one person who could have done this . . . Guy Chalmers."

Jennie stared at him in shocked disbelief.

"My lord," came Mr. Porteous' voice, "I have here an urgent letter from a Mrs. Waring begging for an appointment. She says she has important news for you."

"Burn it," said the Marquis, without looking around.

"Very good, my lord," said Mr. Porteous, and Alice, who had meant to tell Chemmy all about Guy's iniquities, was never to have the opportunity until much, much later.

Jennie was a mass of seething emotions, jealousy being the predominant one. She said, "You were saying, my lord, that there was only one person who could have done this . . . you forget. There is yourself."

"Is that what you think of me?" said the Marquis in much his old lazy manner, although his eyes were like chips of ice.

"Oh, I don't think anything. I have no mind," snapped Jennie. "Yes, I do think one thing. I think I would like to get as far away from you as possible. I shall go to Runbury and occupy my time, supervising things there."

"As you will," said her husband distantly.

He watched her flounce out of the room, his face withdrawn, then got to his feet and strolled into the study where Mr. Porteous was bent over his books.

"Porteous," he said abruptly, "My wife is traveling to Runbury Manor. I want you to go with her and guard her at all times. Send to me a daily report of her doings. I also want you to instruct the servants and my steward not to allow Mr. Guy Chalmers admittance to any part of the estate. Do I make myself clear?"

"Yes, my lord."

"Very good. You may take a break from your work if you wish."

"Certainly, my lord," said Mr. Porteous, his face brightening.

Sally Byles stood in the hallway of her parents' town house and read the little note which had been slipped into her hand by the tutor who had been waiting for her outside her home. It read:

"I am to travel to Runbury Manor with her ladyship. I am distressed to leave this city *which holds all that my heart desires*. Farewell. Andrew."

"Andrew," breathed Sally. "What a beautiful name!"

She rushed in search of her mother and bewildered that poor woman with an impassioned tale of how Jennie desperately needed her companionship at Runbury Manor.

Mrs. Byles at last gave her consent for Sally to go. Mrs. Byles had taken Mr. Deighton in dislike and thought it would be a good excuse to remove her daughter from town.

The Marquis of Charrington called at Mr. Guy Chalmers' lodgings to be told he had gone from town.

Mr. Peregrine Deighton called at the Byles' residence the following day to be told that Miss Byles had already left for the country.

The two friends, Perry and Chemmy, were left to enjoy the sports and amusements of their former days, but somehow the savor had gone.

Damnable women, thought Perry. They ruin everything!

Chapter Ten

The first few weeks at Runbury Manor were surprisingly pleasant. There was so much to do, so much new furniture to arrange, so many curtains to hem and wallpapers and paints to choose for the walls.

The only thing that Jennie found amiss was the peculiar amount of gamekeepers patrolling the grounds. Every time she went for a sedate walk with Sally to supervise new improvements to the gardens, a man with a gun seemed to pop up from behind every rose bush. She had asked the steward the reason for it but he had only smiled and said he was following the Marquis' instructions.

The old servants had arrived to a joyful welcome from Jennie. Their duties were to be extremely light as there was, by the time of their arrival, already an army of servants in residence.

Jennie enjoyed all the bustle and noise and the banging, hammering and painting of the workmen. It also meant that Sally had little time to be alone with Mr. Porteous. Jennie was fond of her tutor but could not help feeling that his attitude to her young friend was somehow rather predatory.

But as the weeks went by and a long period of

rainy weather set in, Jennie's excitement began to wane. Try as she would to concentrate on the fact that her husband was a philanderer and more than possibly a would-be murderer, she found her treacherous body aching for his touch. She was not pregnant and that also distressed her. That splendid night of lovemaking had meant nothing to her husband and she had not even the prospect of a child to console her.

She had not heard from Guy and was strangely relieved. She thought more and more of what Chemmy had said about Guy being the guilty party and she wondered if it could possibly be true.

She also became increasingly worried about the growing relationship between Mr. Porteous and Sally, and wished fervently there was some older person to advise her. Sally was already chattering about how she would inherit money from her grandmother when she was twenty-one and was perpetually telling Jennie that elopements were "quite dreadfully romantic."

Jennie walked into the drawing room quietly one morning and stood aghast at the sight of the tutor clutching Sally in his long bony arms, and kissing her with passionate savagery. She whisked herself out of the room and stood in the hall. "What shall I do?" she prayed. "Dear God, let something happen to stop this." Feeling very young and bewildered and alone she ran to her room and indulged in a hearty bout of tears and then lay prone on the bed and *ached* for her husband. "I don't care if he wants to kill me," she muttered into the uncaring pillow. "I shall write and *beg* him to come to me."

After some time, she rose and dried her eyes. The problem that was Sally and the tutor must be faced. She was, after all, as a married woman, Sally's chaperone and she must not be put off from her duty by her own lack of years. She would speak sternly to Sally and, if Sally would not listen to her, then she would write to Mr. and Mrs. Byles.

She marched firmly down the stairs. Galt, Runbury Manor's new butler, a thick-set individual of awe-inspiring stateliness, waylaid her in the hall.

"There is a young lady to see you, my lady," said Galt with a strange tinge of amusement in his voice. "I have put her in the Blue Saloon."

"Did she give a name?"

"Oh, yes, my lady. A Mrs. Porteous."

"Mrs. *Porteous?* A *young* lady!" exclaimed Jennie, and then carefully schooling her features, she said, "very good, Galt. I will see her immediately."

Galt bowed and threw open the double doors leading to the now refurbished Blue Saloon.

The lady standing by the empty fireplace seemed very young but, as she walked forward, Jennie noticed that she was, in fact, somewhere in her thirties.

She had a thin, pale face and pale, myopic eyes. She was dressed in a plain round gown of gray alpaca and from under the brim of her severe bonnet, wisps of red hair escaped.

She spoke in a clear, well-bred English voice, "My lady, the Marquis of Charrington, your husband, told me I should find Mr. Porteous here. He wished to write to you to apprise you of my coming but I said to him, I said, 'Nay, my lord, I wish to surprise my Andrew.' The Duke of Westerland is anxious to secure Andrew's services again and, after receiving a letter from your husband, His Grace kindly suggested I should travel to England to fetch my husband."

"Mr. Porteous is your husband," said Jennie flatly. It was not a question.

"Oh, yes, my lady," said Mrs. Porteous. "We have been married these past ten years and have two fine boys. I was lady's maid to Her Grace, the Duchess of Westerland, when I met Andrew. I hope it is not an imposition, my arriving like this?"

"No. Oh, no," said Jennie faintly. She tugged at the bell rope.

When Galt appeared, Jennie said: "Pray inform Mr. Porteous that there is a *lady* to see him. Do not tell him that his visitor is Mrs. Porteous. Mrs. Porteous wishes to surprise him." Jennie did not want Sally to overhear and so receive the shocking news from a servant.

"Quite, my lady," said Galt. "I do understand."

Jennie sat very tense, listening to a murmur of voices in the hall. Then, to her dismay, she heard

Sally cry, "Dear Andrew, is this perhaps one of your fair charmers? A rival for your affections?" and Mr. Porteous' deep answering laugh.

Galt said something in a low voice and Mr. Porteous' answer rang out clearly, "Nonsense, man. Whoever the leddy is I am sure Miss Byles is as anxious to discover who it is as I am."

The doors swung open and Mr. Andrew Porteous stood on the threshold with Sally's hand on his arm.

He looked straight across the room at his wife and his face turned a dull red. Sally, who had begun by smiling brightly, slowly looked from one to the other and her smile slowly faded.

"You are looking very well, Andrew," said Mrs. Porteous, walking forward and kissing him on the cheek. She seemed completely unaware of the consternation on her husband's red face and the white-faced dismay on Sally's. "Isn't this a lovely surprise? I have his lordship, the Marquis of Charrington's traveling carriage outside, ready to convey us to London and from thence to the north. The Duke is anxious to have you back, Andrew. Now, we shall just go to your room and start your packing."

Mr. Porteous pulled himself together with a great effort. "I am glad to see you, Abigail. You have met her ladyship already. May I present Miss Byles, a guest of her ladyship?"

Mrs. Porteous sank into a deep curtsey but her rather vague eyes never left her husband's face. "The boys will be glad to see their Papa," she went on. "Come, Andrew."

She curtsied to Jennie and again to Sally and then drifted from the room. "Come, Andrew," she said again, her light colorless voice floating in from the hall.

Mr. Porteous took a step towards Sally, who immediately backed away, staring at him, her blue eyes wide with shock.

"Ah, weel," quoted Mr. Porteous with a heavy sigh. " 'How happy could I be with either, were t'other dear charmer away.' Aye, just so."

With that, he walked heavily from the room. Both girls stood staring at each other, listening to the slow, heavy tread of his footsteps as he followed his wife upstairs.

"Jennie!" whispered Sally desperately.

"No!" said Jennie fiercely. "Not here. Do not let the servants see your distress. We shall go outside to the garden."

Both girls left the room in silence and met again in the hall, after they had changed into long cloaks and put calashes over their bonnets to protect them from the rain and heavy wooden pattens over their slippers.

In silence they walked around the side of the house, down a few mossy steps into the rose garden and along a cinder path where an antique sundial dripped rainwater like tears, as if mourning the loss of sunny days.

The sky seemed to press down upon the house, flat and sodden and gray. The rose garden was very still and silent except for the steady patter of rainwater falling on the leaves.

"Now, Sally . . ." said Jennie.

"He promised to marry me," said Sally, her voice a dismal echo of the gray weather.

"Did he exactly *promise?*"

"Not in so many words. Just things like we should spend our days in each other's arms. I feel *dirty.*"

"You didn't . . . I mean, you couldn't . . ." began Jennie.

"Lose my maidenhead, you mean," said Sally with a harsh laugh. "No, thank God. Oh, Perry, how I have misjudged you."

"Does Perry come into this?" queried Jennie.

"He has written to me every day," said Sally in a low, intense voice. "Long, long letters of love and devotion and Andrew and I used to read them together and *laugh* at them and sometimes I would feel ashamed and start to defend Perry and then he, Andrew, would take me in his arms and make love to me and I would forget everything else. What am I to do, Jennie? I'm so ashamed."

The tears dripped down Sally's face and the rainwater dripped down the sundial and water ran down Jennie's cloak and dripped inside her pattens and she felt she had never been so young or helpless before.

"You must stay out of the road until Mr. Porteous leaves," said Jennie at last. "He is not worth crying over. You know, Sally, when you were so upset about Perry choosing your trousseau, you should have told him so and then tried to work something out. And I . . . I should have told Chemmy all about the Charrington diamonds. I should have told him I was never really in love with Guy. But I'm frightened . . . frightened in case I tell him and . . . and it turns out to mean nothing to him after all.

"I'm in love with him, I'm frightened he will never love me . . . I'm frightened he is trying to kill me. He said Guy was the one who put that spike in my saddle but then . . . that awful man in Vole Lane said Chemmy had paid him. But how can one love someone and still believe that person to be a villain? Chemmy is so easy-going and amiable and yet he sometimes betrays an intensity which frightens me. And I don't understand Guy any more. He somehow seems shallow and I know now that it was a shocking thing to do to suggest I should set up a flirt. I don't know what to do. You're not listening to a word of this, poor Sally. Shall we try to bring our gentlemen here? Shall we have a ball? Shall we, Sally? We'll invite all the county and send to London for Perry and Chemmy and we'll wear our prettiest ball gowns and you shall forget that dreadful Mr. Porteous."

"I-I don't care about *anything*," wailed Sally. "I'm going to die."

"No, you're not, you silly goose. Come with me now and we shall go to the greenhouses and steam ourselves dry and admire the fruit and so pass the weary time. I shall not take my leave of

171

Mr. Porteous. He was a very good tutor and I am grateful to him for saving my life but he has abused my hospitality by trying to seduce my friend and I feel too young and embarrassed to cope. Oh, why isn't Chemmy here! He should have guessed the appearance of Mrs. Porteous would be a dreadful shock!"

"Shock tactics, that's why," said the Marquis of Charrington, smiling at his friend Perry's agitated face. "And it worked, did it not? Sally has written begging you to attend the ball."

"But to trust your wife and Sally alone with a man *known* to be a philanderer . . ." began Perry.

The two men were seated in the Marquis' drawing room.

Chemmy smiled. "It seems that our Mr. Porteous was nothing but a harmless ladykiller who received every encouragement from Sally. I already knew enough of his character to know that, despite this one shortcoming, he would make an ideal watchdog for my wife."

"And an ideal seducer for my fiancée," grated Perry.

"Cheer up, man," said the Marquis. "It has all worked out for the best. If I do not seem overmuch concerned about your worries, it is because I have many of my own. I received a letter this morning from Alice Waring. It seems that Guy Chalmers plotted to ruin Jennie so that he might inherit the grandfather's estate and, having failed to do that, has been trying to keep myself and my wife at loggerheads so that we do not produce heirs. I also believe he has been trying to murder her. Although Jennie's attacker in Vole Lane failed in his mission, it was a stroke of genius to accuse me of being behind the attempt.

"At first I thought Chalmers was simply trying to seduce Jennie and I even gave him the credit for being in love with her! Later I began to suspect he might be playing a deeper game. I have been very unfair to Jennie and now I fear for her safety. Had I thought for a minute that Chalmers was such a villain I would not have waited in the wings so calmly, letting things take their course."

"I shall call him out!" said Perry, leaping to his feet.

"No, no," said the Marquis. "Sit down, my fire-eating friend. We shall draw him. Jennie has added a postscript to her letter telling me that Guy has not been invited to the ball. You and I, my friend, shall go in search of Mr. Chalmers and I shall let him know that I am about to terminate this marriage of convenience and turn it into a love match. We shall tell him of the ball. I shall tell my steward to call off the guards at Runbury Manor and mark my words, Guy will turn up on the night of the ball, hell-bent on murder. Jennie will never believe my accusations unless he is unmasked before her eyes for the villain that he is."

"But Chalmers has gone to earth," said Perry. "No one has seen him about."

"I have news from my spies," said Chemmy,

"that he has been frequenting the gin palaces of Tothill. We shall no doubt find him there. We shall be very friendly and a shade patronizing and a little bit triumphant. That should get him."

"You are exposing your wife to a great deal of danger," said Perry severely, but the Marquis only laughed. "She will be closely guarded, I assure you. I feel this comedy of errors is drawing to a close. There is nothing like old-fashioned marriage, after all, Perry. You should try it."

"I mean to," said Perry grimly. "But first let us hunt down the elusive Mr. Chalmers . . ."

The rain hammered relentlessly down on the mean and narrow streets of Tothill, one of London's less salubrious areas.

"Is there no end to this search," complained Perry. "My very clothes are beginning to stink. We have crawled in and out of a dozen low kens these past two hours and have seen neither hide nor hair of Mr. Chalmers."

"Patience," was all the Marquis would say. Perry looked at his big friend. The Marquis appeared to have recovered all of his unflappable amiability. His morning dress was as exquisite as ever and, in fact, his attire looked more suitable for paying a call on Carlton House than for searching around the stews of this most depressing of areas, where the occupants lurched around the streets in the last stages of rags and filth and degradation.

Perry could only be thankful that the Marquis

had decided to make his search in his closed carriage.

At last the Marquis rapped on the roof of the coach with his cane and the carriage lurched to a halt.

Peering through the rain-streaked window, Perry saw the red latticed windows of another tavern called The Jolly Beggars. Both men climbed down into the full violence of the rain.

The Marquis bent his head and ducked into the low doorway of the inn. He pushed open the inner door which led to the taproom. "Found!" he muttered under his breath. Perry stood on tiptoe and peered over the Marquis' broad shoulder.

Guy Chalmers was lounging in a settle beside the inn fireplace. A slatternly tavern wench was sprawled on his knee and Guy was absentmindedly fondling her dirty breasts as he stared at the Marquis framed in the doorway. The rest of the company consisted of a group of five young bloods who were also sprawled about at their ease.

"What brings you here?" asked Guy with a fixed smile painted on his face.

"Why you, dear boy," said the Marquis amiably. He looked down from his great height at two of the young bucks sprawled on the settle opposite Guy and said softly, "Do you mind if I sit down for a minute? I am extremely fatigued."

They rose with their mouths open and shuffled slightly to one side.

"So kind," said Chemmy, carefully dusting the settle with his handkerchief and sitting down. "And now my dear Guy. I have *very* good news for you. I know your concern for Jennie and I know you will be pleased. We have decided to terminate our marriage of convenience."

"Divorce?" said Guy eagerly, pushing the dirty female off his lap so that she fell with a bump on the floor.

Chemmy raised his thin eyebrows. "Of *course* not," he said earnestly. "On the contrary. Jennie and I have discovered that we are . . . er . . . *very* much in love."

"Why are you telling me this?" said Guy harshly.

"To put your mind at ease," said Chemmy, stretching out his long legs and sinking his hands deep in the pockets of his coat. "You have often told me how fond you are of her. So now you need have no more worries. She is happy and very much in love. We celebrate our bliss at this ball Jennie is holding at Runbury Manor."

"So *that* is why she wrote to me and told me I must not attend," said Guy savagely.

"She did?" The Marquis looked much amused. "Pity. But no doubt we shall see you around on some other occasion. I hope you do not object if we take our leave, Chalmers." He took out a scented handkerchief and held it delicately under his nose. "The air in here is a trifling strong for me."

Guy leaned back in the settle and said softly,

"You have indeed ventured into a rough neighborhood, Marquis. You may leave any time you wish, but perhaps these others do not wish you to go."

The other young men grinned at his words and pressed closer. One of them pushed his face close to the Marquis' and said, "You ain't going nowhere, pretty boy."

The Marquis took his hand out of his pocket and, shaking back the ruffles of lace at his wrist, lazily pushed the leering face away.

"Keep your distance, fellow," he said good-humoredly. "You stink abominably."

The youth swung an ugly punch full at Chemmy's face. The next minute his arm was seized and twisted and he found to his surprise that he was lying in the empty fireplace, staring up into the Marquis' mocking eyes.

Guy's dirty lady friend let out a squawk of fright and ran out of the inn.

"What's up with you!" howled Guy. "There's only two of them and one of 'em's a little runt."

There was a gasp of pure rage from Perry. Finding himself confronted by two of the bucks, his fist lashed out and bloodied one's face. He then picked up the huge struggling bulk of the other as if he were holding a featherweight and threw him straight across the room, where he crashed full into Guy.

"How *noisy* it is here," said Chemmy plaintively, getting to his feet.

He found his way to the door blocked by the

remaining two, and got rid of that obstacle by crashing their heads together.

"Come, Perry," he said. "An interesting entertainment, Mr. Chalmers."

But Guy had fled.

Chapter Eleven

The sun sparkled down on Runbury Manor and summer seemed to return to the countryside. The old house was in a bustle of preparation for the ball to be held that evening.

Gardeners crossed and re-crossed the hall, carrying huge tubs of flowers. Men hammered and whistled from the south lawn, where a huge marquee was being erected to form a temporary ballroom, complete with polished wood floor. The servants worked with a will, having been promised their own ball the following week. Jeffries, the lady's maid, led small guided tours of servants to view Jennie's ball gown, which had been sent to her by her husband.

It was made of pale rose muslin, so fine as to be almost transparent. The underdress was of intricately embroidered rose silk. The small puffed sleeves were decorated with a tiny edging of small rosebuds and the deep flounces were trimmed with the same flowers. On a special stand on the dressing table were displayed the Charrington diamonds which John, Chemmy's groom, had conveyed to the Manor himself. They had been accompanied by a brief note from the Marquis, who had simply stated that he hoped his wife would oblige him by wearing the jewels.

Jennie had read the note several times, wondering what her husband had been thinking when he sent them, happy one minute that he was coming to the ball, sad the next that he had not arrived sooner.

Sally, too, was disappointed that Perry had not rushed immediately to her side. He had sent a formal acceptance of Jennie's invitation but there were no more passionate lover-like letters.

Both girls escaped to a far corner of the gardens in order to worry together in peace and quiet, each one voicing her own thoughts and not listening to the other.

"It's not as if I really *know* Chemmy," said Jennie sadly. "I've thought and thought about him so much that I cannot even remember what he looks like. Perhaps I should have asked Guy to the ball, after all. But I thought Chemmy would like it better if Guy wasn't there. Do you think Chemmy can possibly be *jealous* of Guy?"

"I don't understand Perry's not arriving before this," worried Sally aloud, not having paid the slightest heed to what Jennie was saying. "Did I ever love him? Did I ever love Andrew Porteous? Oh, I'm so upset and one thing is clear. I must marry someone. I shall be an old maid soon!"

"He thinks me mercenary," said Jennie sadly, watching a blackbird tugging a worm from the lawn. "But he *did* send the diamonds. Has he forgiven me? Or does he think he is giving in to my greed. Oh, dear."

"Oh, dear," echoed Sally, and both girls relapsed into silence.

Jennie came out of her reverie to notice that a liveried footman was crossing the lawn towards her, carrying a long letter on a tray.

"It is probably from one of our guests, who finds he is unable to make the journey," she said to Sally as she broke open the letter without bothering to look at the seal.

"Oh, 'tis from Guy. Ooooh!" With dilating eyes, Jennie scanned the single sheet.

"Meet me on the far side of the lake at ten this evening," Guy had written. "Your husband is trying to kill you so that he can marry Alice Waring. I have definite proof. An' you love me, Jennie, do not fail me."

"What is it?" demanded Sally.

"Nothing," said Jennie quickly. "Do excuse me, Sally."

She ran quickly to the house, her heart beating against her ribs. Which one should she trust? Guy, whom she had known since a child, or the enigmatic husband she loved despite her better judgement. And ten o'clock! The ball would be in full swing and all the guests would be there. *I shall worry myself into a fever if I go on like this,* thought poor Jennie. *I must be very brave and pray that Guy has no proof at all and is simply talking nonsense.*

The ball was a resounding success for everyone except Jennie and Sally. So many people turned up that one was in constant danger of having one's gown torn off one's back, thought Jennie. But society was never happier than when they were jammed together, elbow to elbow.

The Marquis of Charrington and his friend, Mr. Deighton, were still unaccountably absent. Jennie had carefully arranged her dance program so that she would be free at ten o'clock. She looked a stately little figure, every inch a marchioness, with the Charrington diamonds blazing in her hair and at her neck.

One minute it seemed as if ten o'clock would never arrive and the next minute it seemed, when she asked her partner the time, the dreaded hour had nearly arrived.

She suddenly wished she had confided in Sally, but Sally had never cared for Guy and would simply make her usual remark that Guy was jealous of Chemmy, nothing more.

At a few minutes before ten, Jennie slipped from the marquee-ballroom on the south lawn and made her way to the house. She left the diamonds in the care of the surprised Jeffries, explaining to the wondering lady's maid that they were so heavy, they gave her a headache.

Then she collected a long gardening cloak from a closet in the hall and made her way in the direction of the far side of the lake. She was glad she had rid herself of the diamonds, which would surely have advertised her presence to anyone watching from a distance.

The faint sweet strains of a waltz floated on the

warm, still air and Jennie remembered how, only that morning, she had dreamed of dancing just that waltz with Chemmy.

It was odd going to meet Guy in this strangely new and sculptured garden. Even the lake had been cleared of its choking weed and rushes, and a new fishing pavilion gleamed whitely from a small island in the center.

There was a little stand of alders at the far side where she and Guy had once shared their hopes and ambitions for the future. Jennie found a little of her fear and apprehension leaving her as she remembered Guy's tanned and boyish face and all the happy sunny days of their youth they had spent together. Of course! Guy was simply annoyed she had not invited him to the ball and was playing a prank on her. How *stupid* she had been to be so upset and so frightened. She would tell Chemmy all about it as soon as she saw him and make him laugh.

"Guy," she whispered, standing in the shadow thrown by the stand of alders. "What game are you playing?" A tall black shadow moved slightly and then Guy materialized in the moonlight.

All Jennie's fears returned as she stared at his face. Gone was the Guy of her youth. A grim, white-faced Guy stood silently looking down at her, his eyes glittering in a strange way.

"What is this all about?" said Jennie. "Please tell me it was a joke. Please tell me Chemmy is not trying to murder me."

"Chemmy is not trying to murder you," said

183

Guy with a grim note in his voice.

"Oh!" cried Jennie feeling faint with relief. "Then why . . . ?"

"I am."

"What?" breathed Jennie. "You can't mean . . . ? Oh, Guy what a tease you are."

"But I am," said Guy, moving closer to her. "Or rather, I have been trying rather half-heartedly to kill you. Our little friend of Vole Lane was not very successful, although I paid him in full for saying that Chemmy was responsible. Then I was so sure you would break your pretty neck riding. Ah, well. As I said, these weak attempts are over. I am about to dispatch you to your Maker."

"Why?" said Jennie, although she felt she already knew the answer.

"Money," said Guy. "That was *my* money, Jennie. I never thought for a minute that the old fool would leave *all* of it to you. I thought he would only leave *some*, and I thought if I ruined you by seducing you, he wouldn't even leave you any."

Guy fell silent, studying her face. A series of bright pictures flashed through Jennie's brain as she seemed to look back on a Jennie now gone forever. She saw herself clasped in Guy's arms, she saw herself throwing a temper tantrum with her unheeding grandparents, wearing that dreadful wedding gown to make Chemmy angry, holding her breath, sighing for Guy one minute and burning up with jealousy for Alice Waring the next.

The spoiled child that was Jennie vanished, leaving a mature young woman who was determined at all costs to live.

"How shall you kill me?" asked Jennie, wondering that her voice should sound so calm.

"I shall hold your face down in the lake," said Guy. "When your body is found, they will have to assume that you wandered away from the ball and fell in."

"Chemmy will never believe that," scoffed Jennie.

"Probably not," shrugged Guy. "But he cannot accuse me, for I have several loyal witnesses who will swear I was miles away at the time."

"What happened to change you, Guy?" pleaded Jennie. "Remember how much you loved me when we were children? If it is money you want, I shall give you plenty."

"I want it all," said Guy flatly. "I am as fond of you, Jennie as I am of anyone . . . and that is not at all. *I* am the only person I care about, for I am the only person I can trust. The world is based on deceit and lies. If you want something, you take it, and if something or someone gets in your road, why, you simply step over them, even if you have to kill them in the process. No, don't try to run away. I shall catch you easily."

Jennie stumbled backwards, catching her foot on a tree root, and fell headlong on the ground, next to the edge of the black lake.

Faintly, oh so faintly, the jaunty waltz danced

across the glassy surface of the water.

Guy was quickly beside her. He twisted her arms behind her back and thrust her face forwards — down towards the water until she could smell the mud of the lake.

Two large tears fell from her eyes and dripped down into the lake, sending little sparkling ripples curling and widening.

Suddenly the ground beneath her began to shake with the sound of running feet. Guy released her and swung around.

The Marquis, with Perry at his heels, was running full tilt towards him. "Oh, God," Jennie heard Guy mutter, although it did not sound like a prayer.

For one split second Guy stood still, watching the Marquis bearing down on him — the next, he was off and running.

Jennie staggered to her feet and stood trembling. "Chemmy!" she cried weakly, "Oh, Chemmy."

Her slim figure swayed as she was engulfed with roaring waves of faintness. The Marquis caught her in his arms and shouted to Perry, who came running up behind him, "Get her to the house, Perry. I can handle this alone."

"Then run, man, run!" shouted Perry, "or you're going to lose him!"

Perry gently gathered Jennie in his arms as the Marquis ran off in full pursuit.

Guy was running for his life. Chemmy was swift and incredibly light on his feet for so large a man, but fear was lending Guy wings. Guy ran on and on, trying to find his direction in an estate which seemed to have been changed completely from the shaggy wilderness he had once known.

New, formal paths edged with shells ran off into strange directions and bewildering shrubbery. He plunged into the rose garden only to find it completely redesigned. With a panic-stricken oath he plunged straight through the bushes and trees, thorns slashing at his face and becoming embedded in his clothes.

He crouched in a clump of bushes and kept very still, trying to control his breathing and peering around like a trapped animal.

Then he saw his escape route as he recognized old familiar landmarks in the moonlight. He burst from cover and ran wildly out of the rose garden in the direction of the north lawn, on the other side of the house from the ball.

He could hear Chemmy pounding after him, but now Guy knew his way.

He plunged into the tortuous paths of the Home Wood which bordered the north lawn, his heart thudding against his ribs.

Then he saw the wall.

He knew that his horse was tethered on the other side.

He was going to make it after all.

Guy scrabbled to the top of the low wall, his hessians sliding on the thick moss.

Good! His horse was on the other side. He

reached down, untethered the reins and let them drop.

Sure of escape, he balanced himself on the wall and looked back. Chemmy was just emerging, crashing out of the woods.

Guy waved his hand in a mock salute and sprang lightly from the wall onto his horse.

But the thorns from the rose garden, embedded in the tough buckskin of his breeches and trailing briars trapped in the tops of his boots, scratched down the sides of the animal's flanks as his feet searched for the stirrups.

The horse reared and plunged. Guy met one of the deaths he had planned for Jennie.

His head struck against the stone coping of the wall with a sickening crack and then he slid down into the ditch like a discarded puppet.

Chemmy hurled himself over the wall. Guy's horse was still plunging.

The moon in all its glory picked out the stark whiteness of Guy's dead face as he lay in the ditch.

The Marquis knelt down slowly beside him and looked down for a long time at the strangely young and innocent face of the dead Guy Chalmers.

Then he heard Perry calling, rose to his feet and hailed his friend.

"He's dead," he said bleakly, when Perry at last stood beside him. "It's a good thing the Chief Magistrate and the Lord-Lieutenant of the county are guests. We can have this mess cleared up and tidied away before we go to sleep. Where is my wife?"

"At the ball," said Perry, staring down at Guy.

"Good heavens!" said the Marquis. "We must go and get her away if it is not too late. She will be panicking the guests with tales of murder."

"Not she," grinned Perry. "I never believed she would have so much courage. The minute she recovered she was all for running after you. I told her that she should go to the house and I would tell her guests she had been taken ill and that a scandal must be averted at all costs. Do you know what she said?" explained Perry admiringly. "She said, 'Then if I cannot help my husband, I shall do all I can to avert any scandal. Don't be concerned, I shall change and return to the ball as if nothing had happened.' You can trust her, you know."

"I do not need to be told I can trust my own wife," snapped the Marquis, angry because the niggling voice of conscience was telling him that he *did* need to be told.

He felt suddenly immeasurably tired. "Let us go to the house, Perry," he said, "and change into our evening clothes before we alert the Magistrate. We'll get a couple of the servants to move the body to the harness room for the moment. Tell them Mr. Chalmers met with a riding accident. It's only the truth after all. Dear God! To think we shall have to go through the farce of attending this young wastrel's funeral and Jennie will have to wear mourning again."

The diamonds once more flashing on her head and around her neck, Jennie executed a Scottish reel, partnered by an exuberant guardee and thought numbly about nothing.

Sally flirted with so many young men that her parents, who were guests at the ball, were thoroughly shocked.

And then the Marquis and Perry strolled into the ballroom, just as the last chord of the reel was being played. Sally blushed and became very quiet and demure, and Jennie's mind began to race.

The Marquis looked very formal and elegant and assured. He moved towards her, stopping to exchange brief conversation with various friends. At last he was at her side and Jennie found her voice.

"What happened?" she whispered. "I have been nigh dead with fear."

"Fear for me . . . or fear for Guy," said Chemmy, looking down at her, his eyes very blue and intense.

Jennie looked at him, her eyes wide with hurt. "Fear for you . . ." she began, and then clutched his arm. "Oh, here is my next partner. Do tell him I do not want to dance, Chemmy, and please take me somewhere quiet. I feel shaky and my head aches so."

"Very well," said Chemmy languidly. "Ah, Struthers," he said to Jennie's partner. "You must excuse my wife. She isn't feeling at all the thing. Come, my dear."

He put his hand under her arm and guided her to the door of the marquee, still smiling and bowing to the guests they met on their road, and at last out into the blessed quiet and darkness of the summer night.

"We shall go to the house," said Jennie quietly. "I do not want to stay in these gardens this night."

The Marquis did not reply but kept a firm grip on her arm, more in the manner of a jailer than of a husband escorting his wife home.

"Let us talk in my sitting room," said the Marquis. "We will not be disturbed there."

When they reached his sitting room, they sat for a long while in silence, on upright chairs on either side of the fireplace, looking for all the world like a fashion plate from the pages of *La Belle Assemblée*, the Marquis in faultless evening coat and knee breeches and Jennie — who had changed from the now ruined rose muslin — in a white silk sheath with a silver gauze overdress.

"Guy is dead," said the Marquis at last. "Broke his silly neck."

"*You* broke his neck," exclaimed Jennie.

"No . . . much as I wanted to. His horse threw him."

"I'm glad," said Jennie quietly. "He must have hated me for a long time."

"Oh, I don't think he hated you," said the Marquis. "He simply wanted your grandparents' money and you were in the way."

"How could I have been so deceived?" said Jennie, trying to stop the sudden rush of tears.

"What a watering pot you are," said her husband acidly, devoid of his usual good humor. "You were in love with him and love is blind . . . or so I am led to believe." He wondered for a moment how he could possibly be so jealous of a dead man.

Jennie dried her eyes. "It is a pity you were never in love with me, my lord," she snapped. "But, oh no, you were wide-awake to all my faults. But I am not avaricious as you believe. I only asked you about the Charrington diamonds because Guy told me you had given them to Alice Waring and she *was* wearing very beautiful jewels and you *were* flirting with her. And you are not faultless yourself, sir! I believe you discussed me with Mr. Porteous and *told* him you thought I was avaricious, for he kept lecturing me through those damned quotations of his about true love being above the price of rubies or something."

"Porteous was very loyal to you," said Chemmy with a reminiscent smile. "That was why I employed him. His weakness was pretty girls, but never married ones. I found out about his wife from the Duke of Westerland. You see, I knew Porteous had burned a letter . . . it was still smoking on the hearth when I entered the study one day . . . and I knew that somehow it must be from the Duke. So I wrote to the old boy, asking him to reply to my club. He seemed amused, to judge from his letter. He has had to extricate

Porteous from many an affair, but the man is such a brilliant tutor that he puts up with his foibles."

"Foibles," screamed Jennie, her diamond tiara glittering and flashing. "Do you call it foible, sir, to try to seduce my best friend under mine own roof?"

"If Sally goes on flirting and ogling the way she does," said the Marquis dryly, "then any man is going to try to seduce her."

"Well, Porteous was mercenary. He must have been," said Jennie, "for Sally kept hinting that she would soon have her own money and that she thought that elopements were romantic."

"That's Sally," said the Marquis scornfully. "Porteous could have eloped with many a wealthy miss before this, according to the Duke. The fun of the chase seems to be our friend Porteous' obsession. Sally might become older and wiser because of her experience. Do you think I would leave you alone here with a man I thought was not reliable? Yes, I can see you do. "

"Guy is dead," said Jennie. "He tried to murder me and you sit there indulging in a petty family squabble. You have no feelings, sir. You are unnatural!"

"I have very natural feelings," said the Marquis. "*I* feel that the spoiled child I married has gone, to be replaced by a beautiful woman . . . who does not love me one jot."

"And does it matter?" asked Jennie quietly, trying to study the expression in his eyes as the candles dipped and flickered in the night wind blowing in at the windows.

"Ah, no you don't," said Chemmy softly. "You cannot take all the time. You must give a little."

Jennie looked at him doubtfully. Did he not know that after the events of the evening, her courage was at low ebb? Sitting very straight in her chair, she closed her eyes. She spoke so softly that the Marquis had to lean forward to catch the words.

"I love you, Chemmy," she said.

She felt herself being lifted gently up into his arms and slowly opened her eyes. He was looking down at her, his face no longer bland and amiable, but alight with passion and warmth. "What do you say, Chemmy?" she pleaded.

"I was always a man of action," he laughed and he bent his mouth to hers, crushing her lips under his hard mouth and driving a whole world of fears and uncertainties spinning away into delicious blackness.

Still kissing her and holding her tightly, he kicked open the bedroom door.

"Chemmy," said Jennie when she could, "you have not said you love me!"

"With all my heart," he said, smiling down at her in a way that made her heart turn over. He put her gently down on her feet, still holding her very close.

"Aren't you worried about spoiling the shape of your coat?" teased Jennie.

"No," said the Marquis of Charrington, holding her tighter, "I . . . hell and damnation. That man has no soul!"

"Chemmy!" came Perry's urgent voice from outside the door. "Are you there? The Lord-Lieutenant is below to see you. He wants to know what you want to do with the body?"

"I shall be with you directly," shouted the Marquis, and then in a lower voice to Jennie, "He will soon have two bodies to cope with, for I shall surely die of frustration." Then he noticed her white face. The horror of the evening had returned to plague her. The Marquis felt a guilty twinge of impatience. She saw death and decay almost every day on the gibbets, so why must she be so nice in her feelings about her wretched cousin? Then he remembered ruefully that none of the bodies dangling from the public scaffolds had tried to murder her, or had been related to her, and gave her a quick hug and kissed the tip of her nose.

"Come with me," he said. "We shall deal with this matter quickly, speed our guests on their way and return to more important business. Remember, my love, Chalmers died of an accident and nothing else befell. We don't want any scandal attached to your name."

Jennie wondered long afterwards how she had ever managed to survive that night.

The painful business of Guy's death was dealt with and was used as an excuse to put an early end to the ball. Although it was four in the morning, it was a very successful affair and could well have gone on another few hours.

At last, of the guests, only Sally and Perry were left. Jennie and her husband sat politely with them in the Blue Saloon, until it appeared to both that the couple were going to sit up quarreling for the rest of the night.

Sally could not be left without a chaperone and Perry showed no sign of taking his leave. He had taken exception to the plunge of Sally's neckline, Sally had taken exception to his criticism, and both were now glaring at each other and trying to think of the most wounding remark.

At last Chemmy spoke. "You're both right," he yawned. "You flirt too much, Sally, and Perry, you're a cursed old maid, and what's more neither of you should marry anyone. In fact, I don't know how Jennie can stand having you around the house, Sally."

Sally gave him an amazed look and burst into noisy tears.

"Now, look what you've done," shouted Perry. "How *dare* you insult her. Sally is an angel and I only said that about her gown because I was jealous. Any man whom Sally weds could count himself blessed."

"Oh, *Perry*," sniffled Sally. "What a *beautiful* thing to say."

"And you shall not stay here and be insulted," said Perry, raising her to her feet and putting an arm around her waist. "I shall escort you to your parents. As for you, Chemmy, unless you apologize to Sally I shall no longer be your friend."

"Oh, run along, do," sighed Chemmy rudely. "Or are you going to prose on all night?"

Perry silently led Sally from the room, his back rigid with outrage.

Jennie collapsed into giggles. "Oh, how awful, Chemmy. You were so rude!"

"How else was I to put a stop to their cursed quarreling?" grinned the Marquis. "Come, my dear."

"The servants . . . ?" whispered Jennie as they mounted the staircase.

"Sent them all to bed and told 'em to stay there," yawned Chemmy. "We shall not be disturbed."

He moved through his sitting room, tearing off his cravat and coat and leaving a trail of clothes behind him, which ended in a small heap at the foot of the bed.

He climbed wearily into the bed and, to all appearances, fell soundly asleep.

Jennie followed him into the bedroom and stared at his sleeping figure, anger blazing in her eyes.

"If I were Alice Waring, you would not lie so like a great pig," she said loudly, but only her husband's gentle breathing answered her.

Jennie took off her heavy tiara and slung it carelessly over the bed post. "But I shall sleep with you, my lord," she said grimly, turning to the looking glass and unfastening her necklace, "for you are my husband, though you behave like an unfeeling boor. Men," said Jennie bitterly, stepping out of her dress and walking over it in all the glory of one of the latest scanty petticoats.

She sat down on the edge of the bed furthest away from her husband and began to unroll her stockings, suddenly staring down at the arm which had crept around her waist.

"Oh, you cheat!" cried the Marchioness of Charrington as she was slowly pulled into bed.

"It's not *decent*," protested Jeffries, the lady's maid. "They've been locked up in that bedroom all day and now it's nearly night again."

"I call it very decent," said John, the Marquis' groom, who had met the lady's maid when she was taking an evening walk in the gardens. "They're husband and wife, after all."

"But it's my *imagination* that's not decent, Mr. John," wailed the lady's maid.

John raised a callused and tanned hand to hide the smile on his face.

"Come along 'o the kitchens with me, Mrs. Jeffries," he said, "and we'll share a glass of shrub and forget about the carryings-on of our betters. Come, it calls for a celebration," he added with an amused glance up at his master's bedroom window.

"The more they keeps occupied, the less the work for us!"

We hope you have enjoyed this Large Print book. Other G.K. Hall & Co. or Chivers Press Large Print books are available at your library or directly from the publishers.

For more information about current and up-coming titles, please call or write, without obligation, to:

G.K. Hall & Co.
P.O. Box 159
Thorndike, Maine 04986 USA
Tel. (800) 257-5157

OR

Chivers Press Limited
Windsor Bridge Road
Bath BA2 3AX
England
Tel. (0225) 335336

All our Large Print titles are designed for easy reading, and all our books are made to last.